I0538599

Poppy

THE MONTGOMERY SISTERS #2

KAT FLANNERY

POPPY: THE MONTGOMERY SISTERS #2

Copyright © 2018 by Kat Flannery. All Rights Reserved.

No part of this publication may be reproduced, stored in a retrieval system, or transmitted, in any form or by any means, electronic, mechanical, photocopying, recording, or otherwise, without prior written permission from the author.

This is a work of fiction. Names, characters, places and incidents either are the product of the author's imagination or are used fictitiously. And any resemblance to actual persons, living, dead (or in any other form), business establishments, events, or locales is entirely coincidental.

www.katflannerybooks.com

FIRST EDITION paperback

May 16, 2018

Publisher: Picco Press

ISBN: 978-0-9811056-6-6

Cover designed by Carpe Librum Book Design

Novels by Kat Flannery

Chasing Clovers

The Branded Trilogy

Lakota Honor (Book 1)

Blood Curse (Book 2)

Sacred Legacy (Book 3)

Hazardous Unions:
Two Tales of a Civil War Christmas
(*by Alison Bruce & Kat Flannery*)

The Montgomery Sisters Trilogy

FERN (Book 1)

POPPY (Book 2)

For my Readers
Thank you for sticking with me!

Poppy

"Vice may triumph for a time, crime may flaunt its victories in the face of honest toilers, but in the end the law will follow the wrong-doer to a bitter fate, and dishonor and punishment will be the portion of those who sin."

~ Allan Pinkerton

CHAPTER ONE

Outside of Dodge City, Kansas 1884

Poppy reloaded the Winchester tucked between her legs. The pale skin beneath the denims winked at her through the frayed hole in the knee. The slacks had seen better days, and right now the rip was the least of her worries.

When she was on the hunt, she packed light; it wasn't wise to carry too many things that could weigh you down. Nope, she'd brought just the essentials. Except, this time she'd made extra room for a hairbrush and the lavender soap her sister, Fern, gave her when she'd visited.

A bullet whizzed past. Poppy ducked lower. She yanked the Stetson off her head and checked it for any holes.

"Damn it." The bullet had nicked the top, tearing the felt.

She crammed the Stetson back on and cocked her rifle. Her fingers tightened around the handle. The cold barrel rested against her cheek, and she shivered. *Here we go.* She slid to her stomach and inched the butt around the boulder she hid behind.

She'd been tracking the Clemmons gang for two months, and now she finally had them. The lowlifes were wanted clear across the territory for robbing the railroad, but Poppy's debt was personal. The gang had killed Molly Schmidt and her son, Tad.

She closed her eyes for a moment and took a deep breath. She'd never met Molly until coming across the turned-over stagecoach to find the mother and son sprawled on the dirt ground. Poppy swallowed. The horrid sight forever etched into her mind. Molly had been alive when she'd found them, but not for long. After Poppy laid the little boy in Molly's arms, the mother took her last breath. The memory still got to her making her eyes sting and throat work.

Killin' had never bothered Poppy; she'd done her fair share and seen more than she'd like to admit, but what had her up nights was "why them?" The thievin' bastard, Lefty Clemmons, had murdered the mother and son, and Poppy'd make him pay for what he'd done. The rebel outlaws had taken the lives of others too, but Molly and Tad had stuck with Poppy when she'd discovered them ten miles outside of St. Louis.

Her eyes watered. She blinked the wetness away as another bullet whizzed past her head.

"I ain't dyin' today," she whispered and rolled onto her stomach. Her sister Fern's lecture on proper etiquette and language rang in her ears. Poppy had always been a bit to the left, as most folks would say. She didn't take well to rules, and she didn't take to speaking like a lady. Hell, she had better things to do, like kill the bastards who had her cornered.

She aimed her rifle as two heads popped out of the bushes ahead, and fired. She smiled when one of the outlaws pitched forward and fell to the ground.

"Gotcha."

The band of men were hunkered behind a stand of pine trees, which made it difficult for Poppy to see them. It would aid in their escape if she didn't get a move on. She needed to push them out of the bush toward her and not in the other direction.

She scanned the field between them. Aside from a few boulders, including the one she was wedged up against, there was nowhere for her to go. She didn't want to retreat into the forest, couple a yards behind her, until she was sure the gang lay dead.

A bullet hit the rock she leaned on and ricocheted to the right. She peeked around the boulder and saw six riders advancing toward her. Damn it. They knew she was alone and figured her stranded. The horse's hooves pounded onto the ground as they drew closer. Dust billowed above their heads, and she knew without a shadow of a doubt they were coming to kill her.

"Shit." Poppy laid her Winchester down and checked the Colts on either side of her hips. She pulled them from the holsters and gripped the handles with her clammy palms. The forest looked more appealing now, but there was no way she'd make it without being peppered by bullets.

Poppy shook her head.

Nope, ain't no outlaw gonna kill her today. She checked the rounds and clicked them back into place before swiveling to sit on her knees and take aim. She fired. Another outlaw fell from his horse and rolled to the ground. No time to see where she'd hit him, she continued to shoot.

Poppy had five bullets in each gun and she'd fired six of them already. The men closed in. She lifted her arm to aim at an outlaw, when a sharp pain penetrated her shoulder. She fell backward. The pistol flew from her hand and lay two feet from her in the dirt. She inched her injured arm closer to the gun. A searing pain raced up and slammed into her shoulder. She hissed.

A bullet hit the ground beside her hand, throwing up dust. She scrambled backward closer to the boulder. Hell and tarnation. She was in trouble. One gun was all she had left. She flipped open the chamber.

"Damn it. Two shots and a lame arm."

She hadn't thought this through when she'd followed the outlaws from town into the blasted prairies. No shelter and her against six dangerous men did not bode well. But Poppy never shied away from danger, and to hell if she'd do so now.

She glanced around the boulder; four riders came toward her. She leaned against the rock and inhaled—two bullets and four targets. And one damn pistol.

Hooves pounded the ground like a hundred buffalo. Oh, what she'd give for a band of Sioux to crest the hill right now. At least she could get out of that one. Most of the Indian tribes were friendly with her. She could speak their language, and had sat many nights around their fires.

She looked at the Winchester lying beside her. With the injured arm, she wouldn't be able to shoot the rifle. All she needed were two extra shots. The outlaws closed in. She had no time to load the six-shooter.

Shots pinged off of the boulder beside her head. She shimmied closer to the ground. The guns hadn't ceased, but instead of hitting her they flew above. Thank goodness. Another shot, this one from ahead of her. Had the gang circled around and were now coming for her in both directions?

In her mind's eye she saw her sisters, Fern and Ivy, standing over her grave, broken and desolate. Nope, she'd not do that to them. She'd come out of this if she was riddled with bullets but, damn it, she'd not die.

Another shot flew ahead toward the gang. She inhaled, rotated her hips, and rested her bloody shoulder against the rock. If this was help, she'd use it. She peered around to see where the outlaws were. The Clemmons gang had retreated, and she stared at their backsides.

Poppy dropped her six-shooter—the threat of the outlaws now gone—and flexed the fist on her injured arm, almost howling from the pain. Blood dripped from her fingertips into the dirt, creating a crimson puddle.

A rider cantered toward her from the forest where she'd left Milo. She went for her Colt and remembered she'd dropped the gun, which now lay too far for her to grab.

The sun caught a piece of the badge he wore on the lapel of his suit. The metal star shone bright. A Pinkerton. A bloody damned Pinkerton. They were the only ones who dressed better than a judge and wore a badge.

Poppy shaded her eyes to get a better look at him. He pulled his horse to a halt right in front of her.

"You all right?" His voice was rough, gritty, and low.

She pressed her back against the rock and shimmied her way to stand.

"I'm fine." She reached for her revolver.

"Looks like you've been shot."

"Nothin' gets past a Pinkerton." She holstered her guns, the movement causing her agony, but she refused to show him how much.

He dismounted.

"No need to stay. I've got things to do." She walked past him.

"Like what? You're bleeding all over yourself."

He was tall and slim, with wide shoulders and a square jaw covered in a day's growth of hair.

"Go on your way." She waved her hand.

"Where I come from, when a person is rescued from a band of outlaws they say *thank you.*"

"Don't know where you come from and don't care. And I didn't need rescuin'." She slammed her hat on top of her head and walked toward the bluff to fetch her horse.

"What the hell is a woman shooting at outlaws for anyway?" he asked, coming up beside her.

"I'm a bounty hunter."

"You? A bounty hunter?" He laughed.

Poppy dug her heels into the dirt and turned slowly. Her arm hurt like hell. She had no time for this pompous Pinkerton who thought he knew her. She'd set him straight.

"You don't seem to believe me."

"Shaw. Name's Noah Shaw." The corner of his mouth quirked upward.

"I don't give a rooster's tail what your name is. What I'm tellin' you is I'm a bounty hunter—a damn good one—and I've been tracking those outlaws for two months."

"That long?" He pushed his Stetson back. "Most bounty hunters track in less time than that. Might I suggest finding another profession…such as school marm?"

"A school marm?"

"Well, yes—or a wife?"

Poppy stepped closer to him. Raised her good arm and clocked the bastard right in the nose. She had a bad temper—always did—and today was no exception. He stumbled backward but did not fall over, and Poppy smirked when she saw the flash of red dash from his nose. He'd riled her good, but it wasn't the reason she'd lashed out. She was angry with herself for losing the Clemmons and getting shot.

"I don't need the likes of some uppity Pinkerton tellin' me who and what I should be. You, sir, can skedaddle."

"Ahhh, hell. You shouldn't have done that," he said, taking a handkerchief from his back pocket and holding it to his nose.

"I answer to no one, and particularly not a Pinkerton," she huffed.

"Sorry, ma'am, but you answer to the law, and you're

under arrest for assaulting a government official."

"I am not, and you ain't no damn government official." She shrugged off his hand when he reached for her. The motion sent a shock of pain running down her injured arm straight to her fingertips.

"Wrong again. I am a Pinkerton hired by the United States government to track and apprehend outlaws."

He spoke very well, and for the first time since she was a little girl back in Boston, she became aware of her demeanor. Heck, Poppy knew she wasn't a looker. She dressed like a man and acted like one. Had to in order to fit in as a bounty hunter. She could fight better than most men, was a crack shot with her rifle and a quick draw on her Colts. She'd earned her scars—every last one of them—and there was no way in hell she'd let this swanky Pinkerton make her think any less of herself.

She pulled her arm up, and the clanking sound of metal rang. He'd placed handcuffs on her. Shackled her to—her eyes grew big—him!

"Unshackle me. I've got a job to do, and time is running out."

"You've been shot, and you're arrested." He lifted his arm, the cuffs connecting them. "Looks to me like your luck has run out."

Poppy's face heated, and she stomped her foot. She better get a hold of herself or before she knew it he'd be wearing a black eye too.

"We have to get that bullet out," he said, directing her to sit on the large rock she'd hid behind not five minutes ago.

The cotton shirt gave a loud belch as he ripped the fabric up to her shoulder to inspect the wound. He was within inches of her face, and she couldn't help but steal a glance at him from underneath her Stetson. His lashes were unforgivably long and framed by even darker eyes. He met her stare, and she looked away.

He was handsome in a rough, rugged kind of way, but Poppy had no time for men. Most of the men she came across were lowlifes who wanted her body or outlaws who wanted to kill her. Noah Shaw was above her league—and not her type.

"The bullet almost went through the other side. Makes digging it out a hell of a lot easier."

"Great." She pulled her injured arm away from him and stood.

"What are you doing? We need to get the bullet out before infection sets in."

She glared at him. "Don't ya think I know that?"

"Then what are you standing here for? Sit down so I can remove it."

She plopped back down on the rock and grimaced. Days out tracking didn't warrant for good food. She lived off of pemmican and jarred goods. There wasn't much meat on her bones, and she sure felt it as her butt slammed onto the rock.

"I've got a kit in my saddlebag," she said.

"And what saddlebag would that be?" He stared back at her.

Milo. Her horse. She'd forgotten all about him. She stood and didn't miss the grunt from Noah as she pulled him along.

"My horse is tied within the first row of trees over there. I'll go get him."

"*We* will go get him." He held up his arm. The jangle from the cuffs pulled her eyes toward him.

Together they walked through the small clearing of dried grass. The dead weeds crunched beneath her boots, and she cradled her injured arm to her chest. Each step she took ignited a pain so sharp she pursed her lips and held her breath. The bullet had to come out. She knew it, and the thought turned her stomach. It wasn't like Poppy hadn't been shot before, she had. However, most of the bullets had either grazed her skin or missed her completely. Being a bounty hunter was rough work, and she accepted it, but damn it if her arm didn't hurt like the blazes. For the first time since she'd taken this path, Poppy considered giving it all up.

She flexed her fingers. She should've bought the whiskey off the old bartender in Dodge City before she left. The liquor would've cleaned the wound and numbed any pain she'd have. Poppy didn't like spirits, but she'd indulge just this once if it took the ache away.

She sighed. It was just as well. She'd get through this without the whiskey and, come morning, she'd be back on the Clemmons' trail. But, the tug on her arm told her otherwise. She glared over at the Pinkerton. She'd leave him behind come dawn if it was the last thing she did.

"Do you need to stop, sit down?" he asked.

She shook her head and forged on.

Poppy exhaled a sigh of relief when she saw Milo grazing on the grass close to where she'd left him. She loved that horse and couldn't imagine living without him.

Noah reached for the reins and led them back toward the rock and the hot afternoon sun. The forest shade didn't afford enough light for surgery. The Pinkerton didn't waste any time and dug into the saddlebags, jerking her arm upward.

Poppy stood and placed her forehead to the horse's nose. "Hey there, boy."

Milo snuffed and stood still, allowing Poppy the comfort she needed.

"Sit." Noah pulled her from Milo to sit on the large rock. He reached under his black suit coat and revealed a hunting knife. The expression on his face never changed from knitted brows and firm mouth as he ripped the rest of her shirtsleeve off and tossed it aside.

Poppy turned away and clenched her jaw until the muscles in her cheeks hurt.

Noah stared at the redheaded woman before him. She was nothing like the bounty hunters he'd come across in the past. Sure, she was loudmouthed, foul-tongued, and had a right hook he hadn't expected, but that's 'cause she wasn't a man. He'd been tracking her for a little over a month. Noah wasn't sure how he'd take the notorious Poppy Montgomery into custody, but he had a mission to complete, and if arresting her under false pretenses was what it took, so be it.

Luck had turned its tail when she socked him one in the nose. He knew she wasn't mild or meek, and she'd be trying to escape within the hour. He'd have to keep a close eye on her.

"You have any alcohol?" he asked, staring at the bulge of skin in the back of her arm where the bullet wanted to exit.

"Don't drink."

The sun caught on the white streak of hair that lay across her forehead. An inch wide, it was a far contrast to the rest of her ruby-red mane. It sure was strange, and he'd never seen anything like it. How had she gotten it? Perhaps she was born with the snowy locks.

He glanced down and was met with green eyes the color of moss after the morning dew.

"You gonna cut the bullet out or stare at my hair all damn day?"

His face warmed and Noah was glad he'd not shaved before setting out this morning.

"With no whiskey, this is going to hurt like hell."

She shrugged her good shoulder. "Nothin' I haven't felt before. Now get on with it."

He wasn't too sure. She was a woman, after all, and most females he came across just weren't as strong as a man. Hell, even a man wouldn't want this pain.

Noah went to his horse, reached inside the saddlebag and pulled out a flask of bourbon. He enjoyed the sweetness of the drink on occasion and kept it purely for pleasure. Today, however, he'd have to use what was left to clean the knife and wound once he was done.

He pulled the cork with his teeth and placed it into the pocket on his vest. Noah slipped out of his coat and laid it across Bandit, his brown appaloosa. The weight of the Peacemaker hanging from his hips reminded him of the Webley Bull Dog pocket revolver that used to be there. It was the first piece he'd ever owned; the first shot he ever fired, and, with it, the first life he ever took.

"You need the knife," she said, pointing to the sheath tucked around his left shoulder.

He blinked. His mind fogged with distant memories

and the smell of gun smoke. He needed a minute. Hell, he needed a lifetime to forget the things he'd done. Noah inhaled a deep breath.

"If removin' the bullet is making you all queasy, I'll do it myself."

He snapped back to the present and met Poppy's glare.

"I'm fine."

"Well, you sure as hell don't look it."

In the weeks he'd been following her, he'd witnessed Poppy Montgomery shoot outlaws, get into fisticuffs, and beat almost everyone she played in poker. He knew she wasn't soft, or weak, or very feminine for that matter, but she was beautiful and *that* he had a difficult time dealing with. What in hell would a woman want to be a bounty hunter for anyway? She'd always be in danger—not just from the job but because she was a woman. He'd pondered this very thought when he first heard her name and was ordered to be her shadow, but he'd not come up with a single reason or explanation.

"Get on with it," she huffed. Her pale cheeks now glowed red with anger, and the green eyes bore into him like a thousand suns scorching his skin.

Noah pulled the knife from the sheath, then poured the bourbon over the blade. He also doused her arm where the skin protruded.

"You ready?"

Poppy nodded. He didn't wait any longer and dug the tip of the blade into her flesh. Dark blood ran down her shoulder as he probed her skin for the bullet. He could feel her tense against him and knew she was in pain. Noah tried to be quick but realized he'd need to slice the skin a bit more to get the bullet out. Once the opening was to his liking, he dug the knife deeper, angled it to the right, and scooped out the metal ball. The bullet plopped onto the ground.

"All done." Though, he wasn't sure if he was more relieved than she was.

He took the handkerchief from his back pocket, doused it with bourbon, and pressed it against her flesh to clean the wound. He was still shocked she'd not made a sound. He shook his head. She was tough. But he'd still need to stitch her, and he knew from experience it would hurt like hell.

CHAPTER TWO

Poppy sat on the ground and hugged her knees to her chest. The fire Noah had built a few hours ago to warm their pemmican had all but burned to ash. She shivered and huddled into herself. Her right arm lay on the ground mere inches from his, a reminder she was bound to him. The Pinkerton lay fast asleep. He'd pulled out his bedroll and, without so much as a care being shackled to her, within minutes was softly snoring.

Being attached to the damn lawman irritated Poppy to no end. She had to drag him wherever she went, and this evening it included a stop in the bushes while she did her business. Noah did show he wasn't made of stone and removed her handcuffs. He'd taken her guns and placed them in his saddlebag right after he'd mended her arm. She'd cast him a hot stare, still angry over the ordeal. She was never without her Colts, even when she relieved herself. She felt naked without them. Her body was rigid; she didn't like that something might happen and didn't have the means to protect herself.

She gave Noah's head a nudge with the toe of her boot, but he didn't stir. Why had he arrested her? It wasn't like she'd shot him or even aimed her pistol at him. Hell, she'd just tapped him on the nose. It wasn't her fault he was a bleeder. She didn't know him from Adam, had never seen him before in her life, and now they were joined together by a piece of metal and his honor to uphold the law.

She had pressing matters to deal with. The Clemmons gang were probably halfway out of Kansas by now. After Noah had stitched her, they went to investigate how many of the gang lay dead. Four of the seven riders sprawled in the dirt and grass. She'd argued with Shaw to let her take them in for the reward money, but he refused, and they left the outlaws for the buzzards. Three of the gang remained alive, and one of them was Lefty. She'd hoped her bullet had found the leader, but that wasn't the case. Disappointment shrouded her, and she couldn't help but feel like a failure.

She flexed her arm to rid the gnawing ache, but the movement did not help and the muscle throbbed. She needed to be on her way, to be tracking and killing. She pulled her right arm up, the metal clanked, and she smiled when he was jolted awake.

Black eyes stared up at her. She held his gaze until he finally rolled over and went back to sleep. He was handsome. Had nice eyes too, and she couldn't help but notice the square chin and the hard lines of his jaw. She snorted. He wasn't her type. She'd never go for someone like him. He was too uppity. Mr. Prim and Proper with a badge and such. Nope, she'd set her sights on someone more like herself. Someone with a little spunk, someone who…who…

Poppy's shoulders fell. Who was she trying to kid? Most men didn't look at her like they wanted to devour her. Instead, they treated her as competition, as one of them. She was the one to beat at poker or in a gunfight, the quickest draw—the list went on and on. She meant nothing to them. But that didn't stop Poppy from wanting the things all girls did, like a husband and children of her own. With the life she led, it was unlikely to happen, and she needed to face the reality of it. Things hadn't worked out for her like they had for her sister Fern. Fern had found herself a mate, one who was strong and kind and loved her for who she was. Poppy hadn't had such luck back home. She'd only gotten heartache and the yearning to be a part of someone's life like her sister was.

She reached for the necklace resting against her chest. Her fingers instinctively found the key hanging from the chain. The jewelry belonged to Molly, the poor girl. Just thinking of her set Poppy's cheeks to heat and her eyes to water. Molly was so young, so pretty, and her son, Tad, couldn't have been more then five years old.

What would those two have had that the gang wanted so badly? Molly's things hadn't been stolen. None of their luggage had been rummaged through, tossed across the prairies like in most stagecoach robberies. But this hadn't been a robbery. The gang had picked Molly and her son for a reason, and what Poppy couldn't figure out was why.

She replayed her brief conversation with the young woman before she died. *"Get the key to Barrister Paul Malone in Jefferson. He will know what to do with it."* Poppy had sent a wire to Mr. Malone two weeks after Molly's death, and they were to meet at his office in Jefferson City in a week's time. Another dilemma she'd need to figure out. When she'd written Mr. Malone, she reckoned on catching the Clemmons gang within the month, but that hadn't happened, and now her time was running out.

She needed to make a decision. Either she stuck to the trail and tracked the outlaws, or she met with the lawyer from Jefferson City and handed him the key. Poppy's stomach felt as if she'd swallowed a lead weight.

She was never good with choices, especially when it

came to deciphering which were right and which were wrong. She always chose the wrong one, partially due to her hotheaded nature. Now, however, things were different. She'd promised Molly to make right by her dying wish. Poppy knew she couldn't back down from that. She wasn't a superstitious person, and she didn't believe in ghosts and such, but she could not go back on her word to the dead girl.

She blew out a long sigh. She'd forgo her hunt for the Clemmons gang and take the key to Mr. Malone.

She glanced down at the Pinkerton. She'd need to get rid of him first.

Poppy scanned his sleeping frame. She'd bet the greenbacks stashed in her saddlebag were now in the pocket of his pants. Poppy cradled her left arm upward to her breast and carefully moved onto her knees. She watched the slow rise and fall of his chest. Satisfied he was back asleep, she inched closer. She sucked in a breath, holding it within her lungs as she perched over the top of him. With no choice but to use her poor arm to search his pockets, she bit the inside of her cheek to block the pain from her mind. She eased her hand into the pocket of his trousers and felt around for the key.

"Well now, Miss Montgomery. I don't usually take bribes, but I do believe you could convince me." Noah rolled onto his back. He smiled, showing his white teeth.

Poppy's palm cupped around something hard, and it wasn't any key. She yanked her hand out, the pain exploded down her arm straight to her fingers and back up again. She clenched her jaw and exhaled heavily out her nose. She scurried backward as far as she could while still attached to him.

Her face heated and her throat dried.

Noah chuckled while he sat up.

"Can't a man get some sleep without being accosted by a hellcat?"

"Why, you no good, highfalutin lewdster! I never accosted you. I'd rather touch a rattler."

"Lewdster?" His eyebrows shot up. "Rattler? You'd take a snake over me?"

She opened her mouth to answer, but he continued.

"And what is a lewdster?"

"A letch, a lowlife, a—"

"Okay, okay. I get it."

"I should be well on my way by now and not hitched to a Pinkerton for something I didn't do."

"You're still on this? You assaulted a government official. That, my dear, is against the law." He stood, and she had no choice but to follow him.

"You've got to let me go. I've things to do," Poppy said.

"Yeah, so you told me." He walked toward the stand of trees.

"Where are we going?" She tugged on his arm and dug in her heels.

"I need to relieve myself."

"No."

She stopped dead and pressed the bottoms of her feet into the ground.

He turned toward her. She could barely make out the shape of his face it was so dark.

"Either you come with me and turn away while I do my business, or I unzip my pants and piss right here."

Poppy's eyes grew big.

"You wouldn't dare."

He smiled, and the sound of his pants opening filled the silent night.

She groaned. "Fine."

He turned away from her, and she closed her eyes. She hadn't realized how tired she was until now—the weight of the last couple of months heavier today than the others. Could be she hadn't been this close to catching the Clemmons gang yet, and damn it, she'd been close. Now she'd have to wait, get out of the mess she'd landed herself in, and get to Jefferson City.

Noah packed up his saddlebag, all while dragging a very angry Poppy around behind him. He hated being shackled to her just as much as she did him, but it had to be done. She knew things he didn't about the day Molly died, and he had to tread lightly if he wanted to get anything out of the hellcat.

"How do you suppose we ride?" she asked.

He hadn't thought about it. After removing the bullet yesterday, they'd found a bluff in the trees and settled there for the night.

"If I release you, what are the chances you'll run?" He watched her expression carefully.

"I won't run."

"Somehow, I don't believe you."

She shrugged. "Well, Pinkerton, you'll just have to wait and see. Won't ya?" Her long red hair hung free of any twine and lay in unruly waves around her shoulders.

"How'd you get the white ribbon of hair?" He nodded toward her.

He didn't miss her back straighten or the thick lips pull tight.

"I was born with it," she mumbled.

"Like a birthmark?"

"I don't know. It's there. It's always been there. Now, are you gonna take these cuffs off or not?"

"I haven't decided yet."

"What are you waiting for?"

He ignored her. He knew when the cuffs came off she'd run—or shoot him. That was a possibility too, if she could get to her guns. Noah went to his saddlebag and dug into it. He smiled when his hand rested on the rope he'd placed inside.

"The answer to our problem," he said, and pulled the rope out and held it high in the air. Without waiting for Poppy's reply, he wound the twine around her wrists to mimic the handcuffs. Once he had the knot tight enough, he took the long end and tied it to the horn on his saddle.

He could feel the anger radiate off her body. He didn't dare look at her. She'd surely set him on fire with that scorching glare.

"Mount up." He swung his leg over Bandit's back.

She grumbled something he couldn't hear as she climbed onto her horse.

He clicked his tongue and Bandit set out.

"Where are we going?" she asked.

"We're headed south."

"Well, that doesn't tell me much." She swung her long hair behind her shoulders and put the Stetson on. He couldn't help but stare at the shimmering locks. When the sun hit them, the red lit up bright like a cardinal's breast. He'd never seen hair like hers and wondered if she'd been the envy of every girl in school because of it.

"You starin' at me, Pinkerton, is getting on my last nerve."

Noah snickered. Her threats meant nothing to him.

She was wild and crazy, and he was up for the challenge. Born and raised in Boston, by a prominent judge and his wife, Noah had been given every opportunity as their only child. He'd enrolled in the Massachusetts College of Pharmacy and Health Sciences, graduating at the top of his class. But he never opened up his pharmaceutical shop like his father wanted. Instead, his life had been thrust into a nightmare. One he still relived when lack of sleep took hold and the memories twisted in his mind.

Two weeks after graduation, a newlywed and soon-to-be father—Noah and his wife, Adelaide—stood in line at the bank. They'd just bought a home four blocks from her parents' in a quiet upscale area of the bustling city. He remembered the smell of her perfume as she held his hand and nestled close to him. They'd been in their own world that day, so in love with each other and careless to their surroundings. When the door to the bank swung open and shots fired, Noah hadn't been prepared.

The masked men wielded their rifles and demanded entry into the safe. They shot at anyone who moved, leaving a trail of carnage. Noah could still smell the blood, hear the screams, see the dead. Adelaide lay on the floor, her blue dress stained red. She clutched the small bump that held their unborn child. It was then something changed inside him. All the expectations his father had put on him became nonexistent. The path he'd chosen had been cut short within minutes. There was nothing left of the life he'd wanted. As he carried his wife's body from the bank, the only thought running through his mind was revenge.

The day after Adelaide and their baby had been laid to rest, Noah put on his guns and joined up with the posse to hunt down and kill the bank robbers. He lived a life of tracking outlaws and criminals for the next five years, until he was asked to join the Pinkerton Agency. He hadn't realized how much he missed a woman's voice until meeting up with Poppy.

"Does everything bother you, Miss Montgomery?"

She bristled. "Everything *you* do, yes."

She was quite the lady. Most women wouldn't dare say how they felt, let alone insult another. It just didn't happen. It wasn't proper. But Poppy let her tongue fly, and she didn't give a damn what anyone thought. He admired that about her. He knew where he stood—and right now it was in a cauldron of boiling water.

They traveled most of the day, when Kansas City became a silhouette before them. A mile from the state line of Missouri, the city had all the necessities any cowboy, or girl, could need. The rope around Poppy's wrists had chafed and cut into her skin, and the hot

Kansas sun placed a red stain upon her face. She'd had her Stetson to offer shade, but for the last two hours they'd ridden into the glaring heat rather than away from it.

Poppy could just imagine what she looked like. The skin around her mouth and forehead stretched tight and hurt to flex. The red hair paired with the red face was sure to look dreadful, and she frowned just thinking about it. She was tired from sitting on top of Milo, tired of the Pinkerton's no-nonsense chitchat, and tired of the heat. She wanted a glass of ice-cold lemonade, a grassy spot under a large oak tree, and a nap.

She glared at Noah. His horse, Bandit, was a large appaloosa and the rich color of coffee beans. Poppy loved horses. If circumstances were different, she'd have made friends with Bandit, maybe even ridden him.

Over the last several hours, she'd considered a hundred ways to attack the Pinkerton, but none produced the outcome she desired. Noah had her guns tucked into his saddlebags, and there was no chance she'd leave without them.

Kansas City had grown since the last time she'd ridden through. At least they were heading in the same direction she needed. Jefferson City was still a five-day ride from here, but it'd be worse if they'd gone toward Nebraska.

The church was the first structure to greet them as

they trotted down the wide road. Farmers and their families walked along the boardwalk, and Poppy's eyes fell on a young couple crossing the street. The lovesick gaze the man gave his wife turned her stomach with envy.

Noah stopped his horse in front of John's Mercantile and Livery. Poppy walked Milo in beside him.

"I need to send a wire and get some provisions." Noah dismounted.

"If you think I'm staying out here tied to a hitching post like some rented mule, you can think again."

He smiled, and she realized that was the only thing she liked about him. Well, that and his eyes.

"If you promise to be a good girl, I'll take you inside."

Poppy growled. Everything about Noah Shaw set her blood to boil.

He undid the rope around her wrists, and she forced back a groan as the twine pulled at her skin. Dried pieces of flesh clung to the braided cord, and when he slid it away the expression on his handsome face changed to a dark, angry glare.

"What the hell? Why didn't you say something?"

"I'm not no whiner. I've had worse done to me."

"I don't care how tough you think you are, Poppy. I don't hurt my prisoners."

"You arrested a woman for defending herself, and you expect me to believe you have a thoughtful bone in your body?"

"Well, I do, and I don't take kindly to you assuming I don't. I seem to remember you attacking me without being provoked."

She slid from Milo and swiveled her wrists to stretch some of the pain from them. "Then let me go. We are on the right side of the law." She was above pleading, but she needed to be on her way.

"I can't do that."

Poppy clenched her jaw. She tried to count back from ten, tried to breathe deep within her lungs as Fern used to suggest, but none of it worked.

She lunged at the Pinkerton, knocking him to the ground. They wrestled into the street, and Poppy landed a punch to his jaw. She ignored the pain in her wrists and injured arm and fought as if she were about to die. She grabbed his Peacemaker and pulled it from the holster.

They separated, both breathing hard. Poppy stood; she didn't dare wipe the dirt from her face as she aimed the gun at Noah.

"Poppy..." he drawled. "You don't want to shoot a Pinkerton."

"I'm not going to kill you, but a bullet in the knee will get me on my way."

Noah shook his head slowly. "That is still attempted murder. You will hang."

"They'd have to find me first."

"You'll be no better than the outlaws you track. There'll be posters of your face all over the territory. You'll be wanted by the law."

She thought on what he'd said. Her sisters would be so disappointed. She'd live the rest of her life a hunted woman, and no matter how much she wanted to pop a slug into Noah's kneecap, she didn't want to be a fugitive either.

"I'll make you a deal," she said.

"I'm listening."

"I'll put down the gun if you let me go."

"That seems fair."

Poppy heaved a sigh of relief. A life on the run was not for her. She placed the bad guys in jail or shot them—whichever came first. She did not want to be grouped with the likes of them.

She handed Noah the pistol, but before she knew what was happening, he had her swung around with her back against his chest. She couldn't move.

"What in hell?"

"Pinkertons don't make deals. We don't take bribes," he said as the rope he'd just removed wrapped around her wrists once more. "We don't take side jobs. We obey the law at all times."

"You no-account weasel." She thrashed against him. "Your word means nothing."

He spun her around to face him. She could feel the heat as it radiated off of his body. He was close…too close. His chest rose and fell in cadence with hers. Their eyes locked, and something in him changed. His face softened, and his gaze held a longing she'd not seen before. Suddenly, she felt herself lean toward him.

She didn't know what was happening. No longer in control of her emotions, she let him wrap his hand around the nape of her neck and tug her toward him. She felt the quick caress of his mouth upon hers. She couldn't stop the desire as it flooded her senses, and her lips tingled. She closed her eyes while pressing into him.

He stepped away from her. "You need to put some Vaseline on your face before the skin starts to peel." He concentrated on weaving the rope around the pole and pulled on the line twice; each time the harsh movement jerked her backward into the wood.

"You're a bastard!" Poppy kept the hurt from her face and lashed out with all the horrible words she knew. He'd tied her arms behind her, and she growled low in her throat as she thrashed against the wooden post.

"I've been called worse," he said before entering the mercantile.

She slumped against the pole. Defeat swept over her

shoulders, and she hung her head. Having fanciful thoughts about the Pinkerton wasn't Poppy's usual demeanor, and she was shocked at how easily those thoughts had come. It not only surprised her but set her all out of whack. She'd let a moment of weakness overcome her, allowed the flakey dreams better left to those ladies who wore bonnets and dresses. And look where it landed her. Tied to a damn pole in the hot Kansas sun.

She lifted her head to survey all that surrounded her. There wasn't much—a handful of townsfolk milling about, a bank across the street, a saloon, and two other buildings. The church bell tolled. She gathered it must be Sunday. How long had she been on the hunt that she didn't even know what day of the week it was? Time had a way of creeping up on a body, but, darn it, she always knew what day and month it was.

She glared at the mercantile that Noah had disappeared into. He'd somehow gotten under her skin, and she wasn't even sure how it had happened. She wished she could wipe the sweat from her brow. Poppy was tougher than he'd given her credit for, and she'd not fall victim to his nearness again. If he got within a foot of her, she wouldn't second-guess this time and would shoot him in the leg.

The sun's rays pelted her skin. With her hands tied behind her, she couldn't pull the Stetson down further onto her forehead. Damn the Pinkerton for leaving her out here.

She eyed her saddlebag. The calendula oil Fern had made for her was tucked away in a small jar. Her sister knew the life Poppy led and how her skin would face the outdoor elements more than a lady's should. She'd made the special oil for Poppy to lather on her face once a week, or for scrapes, cuts, and burns. The flower took the tightness, pain, and itchiness from her skin within the day of applying it. Fern called it a miracle in a jar.

Poppy smiled thinking of her kooky sister. Fern was smart, and when it came to herbs and flowers, she was one of the best at concocting remedies. Poppy was more like Ivy when it came to lack of interest in Fern's garden, but that was where the similarities ended. The young girl, probably a grown woman now, was shy and quiet. Always had her head in a book and daydreaming. Poppy missed them both.

"I got you a sarsaparilla," Noah said.

She gave him a glare fit to melt ice.

He placed the bottle on the boardwalk and untied her from the hitching post. He hadn't been gone long, and she wondered what kind of telegram he'd sent. Once her wrists were free of the rope, she reached for the bottle. It was cold, and she placed it against her hot cheeks before taking a long drink. She watched through her lashes as he placed the rope back inside his saddlebag.

"They say the drink offers reprieve from a sunburn. Not sure how that works, but it's worth a try."

"You're not going to tie me back up?"

"Only when I can't watch you myself. I figure you won't go anywhere without your six-shooters, and if you try to escape me again I'll shoot you."

She didn't say anything. Right now, she was tired, and her face pounded. The last couple of days had been some of her worst in a long time. Shot, arrested, and now burned to a crisp.

"Are we staying in town?" she asked, a little excited at the possibility of sleeping in a bed instead of a bedroll on the hard ground.

"Nope. We'll make camp a few miles outside of it."

"I could use a bath and a decent meal." She wouldn't beg or push it further, but the week's worth of dust on her skin almost made her do it.

He took a long drink from his sarsaparilla before he answered her. "We would have to share a room."

She didn't think her face could get any redder than it already was.

"You can sleep on the floor." She pushed from the post, grabbed Milo's reins, and walked toward the first hotel she saw.

CHAPTER THREE

Noah glanced at his pocket watch for the third time. Poppy had been in the room a whole hour, and he was growing restless. His stomach growled, and he fidgeted from one foot to the other. The dark musty hallway stank like stale bread. The thought of standing another minute confined to the narrow space made Noah squirm. He didn't like closed-in areas—hadn't since he was a young boy and fell in a den of snakes. They'd been harmless garters, but since then he hadn't cared much for small spaces—or the slithering creatures.

He blew out a long breath and clenched his jaw. He agreed to wait in the hall while Poppy bathed and cleaned herself up before they went down to the restaurant for a meal. Now he regretted the decision to remain in the stuffy corridor, but he knew if he'd left her alone for one second, she'd be gone. As it was, he'd paid the youngster downstairs to keep an eye on the window. Give a long, loud whistle, Noah had told him, if a female with hair the color of fire crawled out of it. So far, he'd heard nothing except the occasional curse from inside the room as she primped herself.

He knocked.

"You almost done in there?"

The door swung open, and Noah took a step back. Poppy Montgomery was a sight. She wore no dress; instead, she had on fitted denims and a clean flannel shirt buttoned to just below her collarbone. It was the same garb he'd seen her wear since their first meeting. He wasn't sure if it was the damp tendrils of hair braided hair down her back, the crisp red cheeks just washed, or the clear green eyes staring back at him that had him blushing like a schoolboy. Hell, he didn't know what it was, but damn it, she set his heart to racing.

"If you keep gawkin', Pinkerton, I'm going to give you another reason to arrest me." She sauntered past him.

Noah chuckled. Pretty as the sky after a long rain...until she opened her mouth. He didn't have to second-guess himself, wonder if he'd said the wrong thing or not. Come hell or high water, Poppy would let him know.

He figured it was from lack of education when it came to the way she was. Probably left to make it on her own since she was a child. It would explain her outward appearance, the roughness, the language, and the way she handled a gun.

He'd heard stories about the redheaded bounty hunter even before he'd been assigned to watch her. She could shoot the hat off your head a mile away, and if she had her rifle, she'd peg you off even farther than that. At first, Noah didn't believe the stories. He thought them to be made-up bull, until he'd seen her take down Henry Morgan, one of the most ruthless outlaws this side of the border.

The fugitive had drawn on Poppy in the middle of a busy street in Little Rock, Nebraska. He probably thought she didn't have a chance, being a woman and all. But Poppy had been ready and faster. She had her Colt trained on him before he could pull back the trigger. There'd been something scary in Morgan's behavior that day, even Noah could feel it, and without so much as a blink of an eye, Poppy shot him right in the heart. She'd taken no chances. Her keen sense of those around her and the outlaws she hunted made her one of the best.

The dining room in the hotel was small and quaint. Five tables sat scattered about the rectangular room, some with four chairs while others had two. Poppy walked to the table by the window and sat.

"Nice choice," he said, glancing through the pane glass out onto the dark street.

"I like to see my surroundings," she said and looked at the chalkboard in the corner behind her. Tonight's special was roast beef with all the fixin's and peach pie.

An older woman walked over to their table, a bright smile on her round face.

"Good evening, folks. What can I get ya?" The tight curls on top of her head bounced when she spoke.

"I'll have the special," Poppy said.

"Me too," Noah replied.

She smiled. "I'll bring the coffee around." She walked away, and Noah noticed the slight limp in her gait.

"She has a stump leg," Poppy said without looking at him or the woman.

"How do you know?" She shrugged. "You've been here before?"

She turned toward him, and again he was taken aback by her striking beauty. How had she managed to elude suitors all these years? It wasn't hard to see Poppy was all female.

"Her left hip sits higher than the right, and if you listen you can hear the wooden sole of the shoe slide on the ground when she walks. I'm guessing she's been on her feet all day, and the wooden shoe is heavy and causes her to limp."

"You got all that from one minute with her?" She shrugged again. "Why'd you get into being a hired gun?"

"I ain't no hired gun. I work for myself." The woman came back with two cups of hot coffee and some milk.

Noah smiled at her and offered his thanks before she left to serve the other tables.

"It's a tough life. Why'd you choose it?"

"I had nothin' else to do." She took her spoon and dropped in some sugar before stirring it around the chipped white cup.

"Married? Children? None of those things crossed your mind?"

She met his gaze and held it. Within the green depths he could see her insecurities. She wasn't all that tough, and he was sure there had been someone who broke her heart.

"Nope."

"Not ever?"

"I'm destined to be alone."

He knew she'd let the words slip. Poppy was a closed-off individual, and to let a stranger see her feelings was not going to happen. But she had no idea how attuned he was to her gestures, her expressions, and the way she chewed on her bottom lip. She'd probably never admit it, but he and she were very similar. Noah sensed that beneath the rock-hard exterior there was a softness she kept hidden, a yearning to be accepted among her peers, and a longing to be loved.

Guilt settled in his stomach, and he swallowed back the truth he wanted to tell her. Trust didn't come easy for Noah, and as much as he felt sorry for the girl, he did not trust her just yet. He shook off the notion to confess what he knew and why he was here, and took a long drink of his coffee.

Poppy eyed the two daffodils sitting in the narrow glass vase on the table. She knew from growing up in a family of gardeners what the flower could do. If memory served her correctly, one bulb of the yellow flower would make you severely ill.

She glanced at Noah sipping on his coffee. His brown eyes stared at her over the rim of his mug, and her conscience screamed to put the horrible thought of poisoning him out of her mind.

She shouldn't do it, but time was running out and she needed to be in Jefferson City to meet with Mr. Malone. The five-day ride was one she'd have to make in four as it was. The trouble with the Pinkerton was not something she'd counted on, and if she waited another day she'd not make it in time.

"Where are you from?" Noah asked.

She didn't know him well enough to distinguish if he

was sincere in his question or if he was just trying to break the silence. In either case, she was thankful. Sitting across from him was most uncomfortable, and she welcomed the conversation.

"I grew up in Boston, and then moved to Manchester, Wyoming." How was she going to pull the bulb from the flower, crush it up, and hide it within his food?

"Why'd you move halfway across the country?"

She scanned the restaurant. Unless Noah had to relieve himself, he was unlikely to leave the table. The waitress placed two steaming plates in front of them, and Poppy put the idea of poisoning the Pinkerton out of her head…for now.

"My mother died, and my father took a job there." She pressed her fork into the mashed potatoes on her plate. The food smelled delicious, and she was famished.

"What did your father do?"

"He was a doctor."

Noah placed a piece of the roast beef smothered in gravy into his mouth.

"Never figured that," he said.

Poppy hadn't taken a bite of her mashed potatoes yet, and his comment stopped the fork halfway to her mouth.

"What does that mean?"

He shrugged.

"Just thought you came from a long line of bounty hunters, is all."

His rash judgment of her was irritating. She'd hoped he was different from all the others who placed her in a category she didn't belong in.

"No bounty hunters—instead, doctors and gardeners."

"I hardly think gardening is a profession."

He was arrogant on a level Poppy wasn't familiar with, and it put her on edge. She pursed her lips. "Well, my sister Fern would disagree."

"Does she sell her vegetables?"

"Something like that." She was reluctant to say more. Her eyes fell on the daffodil. "Are you going to tell me where you're taking me?"

He didn't answer; instead, he shoveled more food into his mouth.

"What am I supposed to do when I get to wherever we're going?"

"Plead your case."

"What exactly am I pleading?"

"Your innocence?" The corner of his lips lifted into a lopsided grin.

"I'm going to ask again. Can you just call it a mistake and let me go?" She tightened her grip on the fork she held.

"Where is it you need to be, Poppy?"

"Jeff— She slapped her mouth shut.

"Who are you meeting?"

He was quick with the questions, and she sat up straighter.

"None of your damn business."

"Answer the question."

"I don't need to answer anything. I owe you nothing, and my life is of no concern to you. So, stick your nose somewhere else."

They ate in silence for a few minutes, then he pushed his plate away and stood. "Are you done?"

She glanced down at her half-eaten meal. He'd gotten her so riled she'd lost her appetite. "Yeah."

She stood, and when Noah turned to leave the restaurant, she snagged the two daffodils.

CHAPTER FOUR

Poppy had a knack for landing herself in trouble, and today was no different. The Missouri sun blistered, and the fact that she was in the middle of nowhere with no shade didn't help. It'd been two days since she'd snuck out of the hotel room while Noah hunched over a bucket emptying his stomach. She'd placed a small amount of the daffodil bulb into the glass of bourbon he'd taken from the restaurant. There had been nothing he could do as she packed up her bag and left him there. He was probably on the mend by now—she hadn't put enough in to make him deathly ill, or kill him. Instead, she'd merely measured the exact amount to incapacitate him so she could leave.

Sweat beaded on her forehead and trailed down her temples. The cotton shirt she wore clung to her back, and the denims drew the heat in, keeping the warm air locked beneath the fabric. The burn she'd gotten while riding with Noah had tanned her face to a golden shade, but the sweltering sun still set her cheeks ablaze. She'd give anything for an afternoon storm, one with high winds and sheets of rain. Hell, Poppy would settle for a few drops—anything to give reprieve of the hot heat setting fire to her face.

She squirmed, the tug of the rope scratched the skin around her neck Flies buzzed in front of her face, and with her hands tied behind her back, all she could do was purse her lips and blow at the annoying insects. Milo shimmied to the side, the rope pulled tight, and Poppy squeezed her thighs around the gelding's ribs to silence his movements.

Milo had a keen sense of danger and had saved Poppy's life many times. Today, he knew she was in trouble. His brown ears lay back flat to the top of his head, and his movements were short and slow. *He must be hot standing out in the middle of nowhere, no apples and no water—the poor guy.* When they got out of this, she'd make sure he got plenty of grub and maybe a beer. Milo loved beer, she didn't quite know how he'd acquired the taste, since Poppy didn't take spirits, but when he was real good, she'd buy him one and watch delighted as he lapped it up.

The inside of her denims were wet from sweat, and she kept sliding down the side of the saddle. Milo's long legs held still as Poppy repositioned herself. She gazed out at the two men leaning against the only structure on the abandoned farm. The Hatt cousins were fixin' to hang her, and right at the moment there was little she could do about it.

The bastards found shade where it looked like an old barn once stood. The beams crossed over one another, but the roof was gone. Sweat rolled down Poppy's forearms and into the rope tied around her wrists. She'd have scars there. The damaged skin hadn't healed from two days before when Noah had tied them together. Poppy tried to pull her hands apart, but the rope was too tight.

Milo remained still.

"That a boy," she whispered.

His ears flicked, and she knew he'd heard her.

He'd stay with her until she gave the command to go, and it wasn't likely to happen anytime soon. She had a bullet to place in Jep's stomach, and another one waiting for his slime of a cousin, Stan. Noah had left her Colts in his saddlebag beside the bed, making it easy for her to grab them and flee. The sensation of her guns tied to her waist always made her feel at ease—like she could do anything. Now they sat on the ground beside the barn and the filthy bugger, Stan. She looked around the field for any signs of a rider approaching.

How had Noah faired? Was he still sick? Had he

given up on his trek to bring her to wherever it was he'd wanted to take her? Poppy knew the answer. The Pinkerton wouldn't give up. He didn't strike her as the type.

She pushed aside thoughts of Noah and looked again out into the open field. No dust billowed above the tall wheat. No sound of horses trampling across the dry earth. She blew out a long hot breath. Not that she needed to be rescued. She'd figure a way out of this mess. She always did. But at this moment Poppy would give anything for a miracle.

"You gettin' tired up there on yer high horse?" Jep asked before he spit tobacco into the grass.

She turned to face the lowlife who'd shanghaied her.

"You're a coward hanging a woman." Jep's eyes narrowed. "You scared I might get the better of you?" Poppy gave the outlaw a wide smile.

"I ain't scared of no one, especially not some female."

The cousins ambushed her upon leaving the saloon in Lexington. Unprepared for the attack, she'd been thinking of home and her sisters when the bastards took her down. The long night playing cards and trying to get information on the Clemmons gang didn't aid in Poppy's skills as a fighter, nor had she been quick enough to grab her Colts and protect herself.

She had recognized her assailants immediately. The Hatts had been trouble since birth. They were out for revenge and, damn it, she should've been prepared for retaliation.

"You made a mistake shootin' my pa." Jep sneered.

"There was a bounty on his head. Come to think of it, there's one on yours and Stan's too." She smiled.

"Shit. You ain't gonna do nothin' strung up the way ya are. And yer a woman. Ain't no woman killin' me." He shot a long string of liquid tobacco through his lips.

The sound repulsed Poppy. She never understood the fascination with chewing on the stuff. It was gross and, worse yet, stained your teeth and turned them black.

She ignored him and worked the rope at her back.

Jep was waiting on someone, and damn it if she didn't know who it was. She went through all the outlaws she'd taken down and their renegade families. Were any of them in partners with the Hatts? Had she come across any wanted papers with details on other outlaws riding with the small group? She couldn't remember. There could be a handful of villains wanting her dead.

She glanced at the outlaw again. He would've hung her by now if he was in charge, but something told her he wasn't. Poppy fidgeted with the rope around her wrists and felt the binding stretch as she pulled her hands apart. She'd keep trying.

"It don't matter much what you say—soon you'll be danglin' from that tree," Jep said.

The cousins had been famous for small-time robbery across the states of Kansas, Nebraska, and Colorado, but it was the killing they did that had the high bounty on their heads. Merciless and despicable, the family-run gang was a bunch you didn't mess with. They'd shoot you with no regret or remorse for their actions.

Jep stepped toward her.

The two looked like they hadn't bathed in months, and they smelled even worse. Jep especially emitted a foul scent, and Poppy had to keep from gagging.

The outlaw placed his hand on Milo's neck.

"It's hot out here, Jep. Can't we just hang her and go?" Stan whined from where he sat.

"We can't."

"Why?"

"You know why, damn it!"

"Who you waitin' on?" Poppy asked.

"You shut yer mouth. I ain't answerin' no questions."

"You and your lazy cousin aren't man enough to do me in yourselves?" Poppy taunted him.

"If he ain't here in the next half hour, I'm gonna show you what a real man can do to a woman." He smiled, showing missing teeth in a black-and-brown tainted mouth.

Poppy's reaction startled even her. She placed her boot to his chest, kicking him so hard the outlaw flew five feet into the air. A gunshot echoed from somewhere, and she flinched holding her breath as she waited for the searing pain of a bullet to pierce her skin.

Instead, the noose fell from the branch and lay limp around her neck. Stan must've accidentally shot the rope instead of her. To hell with it, Poppy was getting out of there. But before she could tell Milo to go, she was pulled from the horse, landing her on her back. The stitches in her shoulder burst open, and along with the pain of her flesh tearing apart, her shirt soaked in the blood.

She couldn't give up now.

The rope around her wrists loosened enough for her to get one hand out. Jep, red-faced, came at her. Spittle flew from his mouth, and bloodshot eyes bore into her.

Poppy threw her feet into his chest again, and out of the corner of her eye, she saw Stan run toward them. With no time to waste, she rolled to the left just as Jep came at her again. Poppy grabbed ahold of his pistol, still holstered; she turned and fired.

The bullet struck him in the belly. She pulled the revolver free, swiveled on her knee, and shot Stan. The charred mark on his forehead oozed smoke as he lay dead on the ground.

Jep's loud moans carried across the field as he rolled

from side to side. She'd take them into Lexington for the reward money after she got the rope off her other wrist.

The distant sound of a horse drifted toward her, and she glanced up to see a cloud of dust coming from the west. A lone rider's silhouette painted the distance. Poppy ran to the barn, grabbed her Colts, and strapped them on. She pulled a six-shooter from its holster and rubbed the handle into her palm. She checked the chamber to see how many bullets remained. It was full. The Hatts hadn't emptied it. Fools. She positioned her feet shoulder-width apart and waited, gun drawn in anticipation of shooting the son of a bitch who was working with the cousins.

The rider came closer. Her finger twitched on the trigger. She held her stance and ignored the throbbing in her shoulder, the blood-soaked shirt, and the pain in her wrists. All her senses focused the man atop his horse cantering toward her. She watched his movements, especially his hands, to see if they went for his weapon. If he so much as moved a hair toward them, she'd blast him.

It wasn't until the horse got twenty feet from her that Poppy caught a glimpse of the badge upon the man's chest.

"Damn." She holstered her six-shooter and walked toward Milo.

Bandit kicked up dust as Noah pulled him to a halt right beside her.

"I should shoot you," he said.

"Count yourself lucky that I let you live just now." Poppy didn't turn to look at him as she saddled her horse.

"Lucky? You poisoned me!"

"I had somewhere to be. You wouldn't let me go."

She turned toward him. He was pale, his skin pasty. He stared back at her through bloodshot eyes, probably from being up all night, sick.

"Sure it wasn't a stomach bug that had you ill?"

"I'm sure."

"How's that?"

"The small remnants of something in the bottom of my glass told me otherwise."

"I ain't going with you."

He growled. "I figured that."

"Good. It's been nice knowin' you, Pinkerton."

"Listen. I'll fill you in later on what I know, but for now we need to ride."

"I told you, I ain't ridin' with you." She walked Milo away from him, but he positioned Bandit in front of her horse.

"Poppy, I know you almost hanged—and we've got about five minutes to get the hell out of here, or we're both dead."

"What in tarnation are you talking about?" She was irritated with him already, and he hadn't been here more than a minute.

"Do you know who Wolf Blackstone is?"

Poppy froze. Everyone in the damn country knew Wolf Blackstone. He was the best hired gun there was. Half Cherokee, half white, he could track a mouse in a field of straw, and he did not take prisoners. His job was to kill.

"There's a price on your head, and he's been hired to kill you."

Chapter Five

"With the two of us, I'm sure we could've taken down Blackstone," Poppy said as they slowed their horses to a steady trot.

Noah didn't agree. Wolf Blackstone was the best, but for this particular job, he'd been using other outlaws to trap Poppy so he could kill her. Which meant the ransom on her head was substantial enough for Blackstone to share, or there was something else pushing him to hunt her down. Noah had been in the saloon trying to locate Poppy, when the assassin walked in. It was only by chance he'd overheard the conversation between Blackstone and another cowboy that some outlaws had the girl just west of town. Noah knew it was Poppy and left without anyone the wiser to his actions.

"I ain't going to sit back and wait for some outlaw to kill me," she growled and turned Milo around.

Noah grabbed the reins to stop her from taking off.

"He's not an outlaw, Poppy. Wolf is just like you and me, except he's better." He placed the warning in his voice on purpose. She needed to see what they were up against.

"He's not better." She stuck out her bottom lip, and Noah had an incredible urge to kiss her. He clenched his jaw instead.

"Yes, he is, and you need to realize that. He's been all over the place killing for money. He doesn't care who you are. If he's paid to do a job, he will complete it."

She released a sigh.

"Right now, we don't have enough distance between us and him. We need to get going."

She resisted his tug on the reins. "Milo, don't move."

Damn it if the horse didn't listen to her.

"You'll have to teach me that one," he said.

"Only works if your animal is loyal."

He glanced at Bandit. He'd never had to test the devotion of his horse before. Truth be told, he figured the animal would always be there.

"One of these days I'll try it," he said.

"I want to know some things." She placed her Stetson low on her forehead, but he could still see her eyes. He liked to look people in the eye when he spoke, and he could tell she was the same.

"We can talk after we get some distance."

She shook her head.

He could see there was no bartering with her.

"All right." He stepped Bandit closer to her horse, took a breath, and told her what he knew. "I've been hired to find out why the strongboxes from the National Bank are being stolen from the stagecoaches within Nebraska, Kansas, Missouri, and Idaho."

"Strongboxes? They carry money, right?"

"Yeah, from one bank to another, and for the past year they've been getting stolen."

"How can that be, with Wells Fargo carrying them?"

"Only a handful of stages have made it through— you know what happened to the others. The Clemmons gang has been hired by someone to rob those stages."

He didn't miss the flicker in her eyes when he mentioned the gang.

"I've been tracking them for a while. Didn't know they were wanted for theft of bank money."

"Well, it's an addition to the long list of felonies they're wanted for."

"There's something else you're not telling me, Pinkerton."

Noah didn't know how much she'd let him in on, and he was tired of the back and forth they'd been doing.

"I needed you." When he said the words they held a different meaning than intended, and it scared the hell out of him. He needed no one—least of all a foul-mouthed redhead. But when he looked at her, he couldn't help the lump as it formed in his throat, or the way his heart raced when she was near. Poppy had done something to him, and he wasn't sure he liked it.

"Well, why'd you need me?" She crossed her arms.

"Molly Schmidt."

She gasped. "How do you know that name?"

"You were the one who found Molly and her son a few months back."

Poppy's full lips gaped. He watched her carefully. Her shoulders sat high, her back straightened, and he didn't miss the moisture gather in her eyes.

"Did you know them?" he asked. The young woman and her son had meant something to Poppy, and he wanted to know why.

She shook her head slowly and removed the Stetson.

"I never met them before that day." Her voice was soft, light. He hadn't heard her speak in such a way before.

"Were you there when it happened, or did you come upon them afterward?"

"Afterward."

"What did you find? Was there any money on the stage?"

She shook her head.

"Nothing had been taken. It wasn't a robbery…"

"What do you mean?"

"Molly and Tad were killed for some other purpose, but it wasn't for money."

"Tell me what else you know."

She glanced at him, and he watched as her whole appearance changed. The once remorseful face turned hard and angry. The lips he had wanted to kiss lay flat and unmoving, and her green eyes became vacant.

"We need to get a move on if we're to put some space between us and Blackstone." She clicked her tongue, and Milo took off. Noah had no choice but to follow her. She had avoided his question like a deer steered clear of a den full of bears. Poppy knew something he didn't, and he'd need to tread lightly if he was to find out what.

Poppy huddled into her blanket and slid closer to the fire. The cave nestled on the side of a hill was big enough for the two of them and their horses, but the secluded hideaway was damp and she'd caught a chill.

"This will help," Noah said as he placed his bedroll around her shoulders.

Her teeth chattered as she huddled into the blanket.

He sat across from her and placed another log on the fire. "I can't help but think this is payback." She lifted an eyebrow. "For you poisoning me."

She gave him a small smile. There was no point in denying it any longer.

"What did you use?"

"A daffodil."

He scrunched his brows, and she knew he was trying to place where she'd get such a flower.

"They were on the table in the restaurant," she said.

"What I can't figure out is how you knew what it did."

"I told you, my sister is a gardener."

"A vegetable gardener, yes." He picked up a twig and placed it in his mouth, letting the end stick out like a cigarette.

"And a collector of herbs, flowers, and roots."

"Why would anyone want to waste their time with such things?"

"For a Pinkerton, you're not very smart."

He flexed his jaw.

She struck a nerve. It was clear he didn't take kindly to being told he'd possibly missed information she'd relayed, but Poppy didn't lie.

"I'm good at my job." He tossed the stick from his mouth into the flames.

"You need to pay better attention to what people tell you."

"And what exactly did I miss?"

"I told you my sister was a gardener, and it was her job."

"Yeah, and…?"

"And she heals people with the things she grows."

"Bull."

"It's true."

"If what you're saying is true, what does that make her?"

"Well, to some, better than a doctor."

He pushed his hat back. "You don't say?"

Poppy nodded. Her sister was one of the smartest people she knew. The things she could do with her plants and vegetables were amazing.

"I take it you learned how to poison people from her?"

"Fern wouldn't harm a fly. The daffodil has other elements to it that can heal."

"Such as?"

"It not only induces vomiting, as you already know, but its petals can be used as a poultice for burns or wounds."

"Which reminds me, how's your arm?"

She hadn't thought about the torn flesh in a while. The aching had ceased, the blood now dried to her shirt and skin.

"Did you tear it open?" he asked.

"I think so."

He went to his saddlebag and came back with a white cloth and a bottle of brandy.

Poppy glanced at him.

"I won't be drinking this stuff for a while, thanks to you, but it does come in handy for cleaning wounds." He soaked the cloth in the liquor. "You're going to need to take your shirt off."

"The hell I will." She leaned away from him.

He laughed. "Relax, Red, just the shoulder."

She wrapped the two blankets around her bosom securely before removing her arm from the flannel shirt. The cotton stuck to her skin. She was just about to yank the fabric away when Noah's fingers lay over top of hers.

"Let me help you." He gently pulled the shirt from her skin.

The slow caress of his fingers traced down the side of her neck to the middle of her arm, and she shivered. She'd never been touched so intimately before and wondered why he'd done it. She closed her eyes while he cleaned the blood from her skin and inspected the wound.

"You've busted open the stitches." He pressed the cloth deeper into her skin. "The bleeding has stopped, but that doesn't mean you won't get an infection."

"I saw some pine trees when we rode in. The sap will pull all the poison from the wound while healing it."

He ripped a piece of the cloth to take with him and disappeared into the darkness without another word.

Poppy waited until he'd been gone for a couple of minutes before allowing her head to hang and the tears to flow from her eyes. She was exhausted, and she couldn't contain her emotions any longer. Little sleep, the pressure to fulfill her promise to Molly, the disappointment of letting the Clemmons go, being hunted by Wolf Blackstone, and the desire Noah stirred inside of her all came toppling down. A sob hiccupped from her lips. She hunched forward and cried softly into her hands.

She didn't hear Noah come back and was startled when his arms wrapped around her shoulders. He pulled her into his chest. She had no energy to fight him. Strong arms held her to him, and instead of refusing the comfort he offered, she placed her head on his shoulder. Not accustomed to this type of affection, her first instinct was to get angry with him, but she ignored the anxiety it brought, knowing she'd not have this moment with him again.

Poppy felt his lips brush her temple and then the top of her head as he offered her his silent support. She sank into his arms, hiding her face from the desire she knew showed there. Her cheeks heated, and she blinked several times in an effort to bring herself back to the reality of what her life was really like. She'd never felt more than a pawn to any man and wondered if Noah was different from the one experience she'd had when she was younger. Would he take from her, only to leave and never return? The thought scared her to death.

She drew her body away from his, but he tightened his arms and again she sank into him.

She wasn't the kind to be put into a delicate situation; she was upfront and forthright, to a fault sometimes, but always honest. Should she ask him his intentions? But what if they were merely to comfort her and nothing more? She'd look like a simpleton. Another tear slipped through her lashes. She'd been alone far too long. Five days with the Pinkerton, and she wanted to have his children. She was being ridiculous. The heat from the fire warmed her, and she yawned. Noah's arms remained around her, holding her tight to him as she drifted off.

Noah knew the minute she'd fallen asleep. The stiffness evaporated from her body, and she sank into him. He welcomed the heaviness that came with her leaning against his chest. He took a moment to appreciate what she had given him. His heart beat stronger just knowing this gritty girl needed him even if only for the night. He had no clue what had made her cry, but the shock of seeing her fall apart was unnerving and uplifting at the same time. Poppy Montgomery was not so hard. She was soft and delicate, and when he held her in his arms, he couldn't help but dream of fonder things.

A sudden urge to protect her at all cost came over him. He brushed his lips across her temple. She smelled of wood smoke, lilacs, and sunshine. He brought her closer. He knew he should lay her down beside the fire and make himself something to eat, but he didn't want to release her from his arms just yet. He hadn't been this content in a long while, and holding her had felt better than he'd imagined it would. She needed him, even if for a short while.

He remembered her wound, and the pinesap he'd gotten to place over it. Without waking her, he slowly laid her onto the ground before pulling the blanket away from her arm. He tenderly cleaned the wound again with the brandy-soaked cloth before he lathered the gash with the pinesap. Once done, he reached for the blanket wrapped around her breasts to cover her up. That's when he spotted the necklace and the small key attached to a chain.

He'd been searching for a key. The one Molly Schmidt had taken with her. The same one that held all the answers the Pinkertons needed. Was this the same key? Had Poppy stolen it from the girl? Poppy didn't strike him as the type that would take something that didn't belong to her. So why did she have it? Had the girl given it to her? Was that the reason she needed to get to Jefferson City?

Noah knew if he breached his assignment he could lose his job. His task had been simple: find Poppy Montgomery, see if she had the key and what she knew about locating Molly and Tad; if she didn't have the key, report back to headquarters.

Wolf Blackstone hunted Poppy, and Noah knew, like everyone else, the gunman would stop at nothing to kill her.

He brought the blanket up to her chin, covering the necklace. Red hair framed her tanned skin. Lush lips, high cheekbones, and a pert chin called to him. He couldn't leave her to that fate, and yet he needed the key.

He stared down at her and ran his fingers along the line of her jaw. She needed his help. If something happened to her.... His heart quickened, and the breath in his throat stilled. It was then he knew—Poppy Montgomery had taken a piece of his soul.

Chapter Six

Poppy leaned her hip against the hitching post outside of the mercantile. They'd finally crossed into Missouri five hours after leaving the cave. It was a relief to be heading in the right direction toward Paul Malone, where the weight she'd carried could finally be lifted. She glanced at the wooden sign staked into the hard earth: Welcome to No Where.

A sad welcome it was. The town of No Where, Missouri, was about as welcoming as a rattler in the hayloft. One saloon, a mercantile, and some tents were the only structures within the settlement. In the five minutes she'd stood there, no one had walked by. Three cows grazed on the grass between some of the tents, and she wondered if anyone was sleeping under the makeshift homes. With no mountains or hills, this was unlikely a mining settlement or trading post. Come to think of it, she wasn't sure what this little town was.

Throughout her years of traveling across the country she'd been through many quaint settlements, but this was not one of them. Something was off here in No Where. She just didn't know what.

She could've kept riding right past this forsaken lot, but Noah needed to wire the agency an update. He stifled her argument, warning her in a deadly tone this was his job and, unlike her, she answered to the agency. Instead of going inside with him, she chose to remain out in the sun.

She pulled the Stetson lower onto her forehead to conceal half of her face. A light wind blew at the nape of her neck, and the hairs stood.

She glanced at the door of the mercantile. Noah had been in there for more than five minutes, so someone must be inside helping him. The shuffling of feet carried toward her, and she scanned the street for the source. Poppy knew from experience to always be ready, be alert. She ran the tips of her fingers along the handle of her Colts. Where was Noah? Why was it taking so long for him to send a wire?

She stepped toward the mercantile, when the faint click of a barrel cocked. A pistol trained on her. Damn it. She didn't know what direction the bastard aimed from either. She tipped her head to conceal her eyes and searched the corners of the buildings, the tents, and the bush to her left. She saw nothing. No movement. No shadow. No gun.

The narrow porch off the mercantile carried past the building about two feet. It was her best shot at cover.

She dove over the hitching rail at the same time a shot went off. Poppy rolled behind the boardwalk. The bullet had struck part of the heel on her boot, removing half the wood from the bottom. There wasn't much room beside the mercantile to protect herself from the shots she knew were about to fly.

She huddled into the side of the building, pulled her guns, and peeked over the porch floor.

If Noah was smart, he'd stay inside. She didn't know how experienced the Pinkerton was in gunfights; Poppy, on the other hand, wasn't fazed. She didn't need him going off and shootin' up the place. It was best for him to stay out of her way, but somehow she knew that wasn't going to happen.

Whoever had fired was a damn good shot. If she hadn't dove for cover, the bullet surely would've hit her. Poppy gripped the handles of her Colts and rolled her wrists. She inhaled deep within her lungs, rested the barrel of each revolver to her cheeks, and said a silent prayer. Back pressed to the wall, she slid up the mercantile and peeked over the wooden walkway.

The gunman remained quiet. Most outlaws would unleash a hail of bullets on her, too inexperienced to wait. The silence told her the shooter wasn't an outlaw but a trained assassin—and had the patience to wait her out.

"What's the plan, Red?" Noah asked from beside her.

She just about jumped out of her skin.

"Don't sneak up on me like that. You're lucky I didn't shoot you."

"You're smarter than that."

Where had he come from? She opened her mouth to ask, but he must've seen the shocked look on her face and decided to tell her.

"This isn't my first gunfight." He smiled. "I snuck out the back."

She watched as he checked the chamber of his Peacemaker, spinning the round until it clicked back into place.

"No plan, except shoot back," she said.

"Well, that would be great if we knew where he was." He tugged his hat down.

"There could be more than one shooter," she said more to herself than him.

"Yeah, you may be right."

"Did you send your telegram?"

"I did not." He looked around. "Odd town. There was only one person working in the mercantile, and I didn't see anyone else around."

"I feel the same way."

They looked at each other. Wolf Blackstone was the only person they knew who could send a whole town into hiding.

"How did he know we'd come here?" she asked.

"Luck." Noah spun the revolver with his index finger. "Ready to get the hell out of here?" he asked her.

"I was ready five minutes ago."

"Can you speculate a direction the shot came from?"

Poppy couldn't say for sure, so she had to wager a guess, "The saloon?"

"Are you asking me or telling me, hellcat?"

She chewed on her bottom lip. She didn't want to give him the wrong information and have him shot because of her mistake. She'd never done that before. Accuracy was why she was so good at her job, but today something had changed. Poppy wasn't sure if it was the trust she'd seen in his eyes when he stared at her or that she'd allowed her heart to fall for him—either way she wasn't about to watch him get killed.

Noah could see she struggled with the answer. Her being a bounty hunter, he was positive she'd been in this situation before. Yet, she fidgeted, couldn't look him in the eyes, and fidgeted as if she were sitting on an anthill.

He'd had an odd feeling about the town when he

walked inside the store and no one was there. He searched for the better part of five minutes until he saw a boot on the floor behind the counter. A man in his late sixties with a long white beard sat huddled against the wall behind the booth. He went to ask him why he'd been hiding, when a shot went off.

Noah's first thought was Poppy. Had she been hurt or—worse—killed? Memories flashed across his mind. Adelaide. The baby. Blood. The room spun along with his stomach as he'd battled the black dots clouding his vision. He had leaned against the wall to catch his balance, and waited for the nausea to subside. He needed to get to Poppy. He couldn't relive another tragedy. Once he was composed enough to move, he escaped out the back door and peeked around the corner to where he knew the horses were hitched. That's where he'd found Poppy sitting with her knees up, pistol in hand, hat low, and determination pressed upon her face.

Now that he knew she was okay, he needed to find a way out of here that didn't involve either of them shot.

"I'm not sure if it came from the saloon," she whispered.

He searched her face. He could see how others would be intimidated by her, or even think she was too crass, but to him she was beautiful. A surge of emotions welled up inside him, tightening his chest.

Pistols still in hand, he leaned in and crushed his lips

to hers. She didn't resist, instead molded her lips to his in the same frenzied heat he'd brought. Noah almost came unhinged when she bit his lower lip and sucked it into her mouth. His desire rose, and if he didn't pull away from her, he'd soon be undressing her. The imminent danger of Wolf Blackstone didn't re-enter his mind until he dragged himself from her. She averted her chin, and he knew recollection of where they were had caused the embarrassment to flood her cheeks.

He pressed his back into the wall, steadied his emotions, and smiled. It may not have been the time or the place for such passion, but damn it, he'd never forget it. He glanced at her, straight-faced and ready to shoot their way out of here.

"Hey, Red?"

She glanced at him.

"You about ready to get the hell out of this place?" He didn't miss the spark in her eyes or the small smile she gave him.

"You got a plan?"

"Well, I'm guessing we call the horses and head out that way." He pointed in the same direction he'd first come.

"What if he's waiting for us behind the mercantile?"

He held up his revolver. "Fire in every direction until we're a good distance away."

"Sounds like we got a plan." She clicked her tongue,

and Milo stepped closer to the wooden walkway.

Noah tried to mimic Poppy, but Bandit didn't come. Instead, the knucklehead grazed on the grass without a care.

"Cover me." He crouched low and scooted toward Bandit on the heels of his feet.

Poppy fired in every direction, pinging the bullets into the ground to kick up dust and cause a shield for Noah. He reached for the reins, but they were shot from his hand. The bullet just missed his fingers and tore the reins in two. Bandit reared his front hooves high into the air and danced in a circle. Noah jumped and scurried back to Poppy, as she fired in the direction of the saloon.

"Damn it, that was close." He took a few more deep breaths before diving back toward Bandit. This time he grabbed the reins from the nervous horse and pulled him to where they sat.

"I need to reload," she said, squatting on her heels and snapping open the chamber.

Noah perched his gun on the boardwalk and continued to fire at the swinging doors of the saloon.

"You ready yet?" he asked.

"As ready as I'm gonna be."

Bullets flew past their heads, as Poppy pulled Milo closer toward them.

"He better not shoot my horse," she growled.

"Get a move on and we won't have to worry about that." Noah fired an array of bullets into the ground, the windows, and the walls of the building.

She slid onto Milo and lay across his back. Once seated, the horse took off behind the mercantile. She didn't dare look back and hoped Noah followed. The trample of horse's hooves was enough to jar even the most seasoned of riders, and Poppy was feeling it right now. Her shoulder throbbed almost as much as her backside did.

It wasn't long before she heard the rhythm of Bandit's steps behind her. They rode hard and fast for some time before they stopped the horses by a stream.

"Do you think Blackstone's close?" she asked, her breath still labored from riding. A thin veil of dirt covered her face. When she licked her lips she tasted it.

Noah glanced behind them and took a swig from his canteen.

"It doesn't matter how far we get from him—the point to remember is that he will come."

Irritated with his answer, she gave him a scowl.

"I am aware he will come, but what I asked was do you think he's close?"

"No, but I didn't think he'd show up in that town before us, either."

"We should separate. Throw him off."

"We are talking about the same person, right? Wolf Blackstone will not be confused if we separate. He knows your horse, and unless you're willing to go without Milo, I suggest we stick together."

She'd never leave her horse behind, and his suggestion to do so riled her. She wasn't dumb. Blackstone was coming, and the only way to stop him was to kill him. Her hand went to the Colt on her hip.

"You can't do it on your own," Noah said.

Could he read her thoughts? "I get you're a Pinkerton and all, but I've dealt with men like Wolf, and I know what needs to be done."

"And you think killing him will be easy?"

"It'll end this cat-and-mouse chase we've been on and get me to where I need to be going."

"You're not experienced enough to pull it off." His eyes roamed her entire body, at first scrutinizing, but his gaze soon changed to something else. Something more provocative.

Poppy didn't like it one bit, and she repositioned herself on the saddle. She was not some silly girl with a sack full of dreams he could squash. She knew someone like Noah would never care for someone like her. Nope. He was trying to fool her—trying to trick her into letting him call the shots. It wasn't going to happen. She was better with a gun than he was, and she'd kill Wolf Blackstone to prove it.

"You know nothin' about me and how *experienced* I am." She bit her lip hard not to add an insult.

"I know you're not prepared for what kind of a man Blackstone is."

"What in hell does that mean?" She took off her Stetson and laid it on her lap.

"He's got no heart, Poppy."

"Aw shit, you make it sound like he's the Devil or something."

"He's damn close."

"I've heard all about him—everyone has. He's a hired executioner, a good one. That is all."

"No. That is not all!" The muscles in his jaw flexed. "He kills, damn it! And unless you kill him first, he will find and kill you. He won't stop until he does!"

She didn't know if it was due to the tone Noah used or the words he spoke that caused her to shiver, but damn it all to hell, she was vexed that he'd seen it. Now he thought she was scared.

"I've got places to be." She really did need to get the key to Paul Malone, and now that she was being hunted, getting it there was proving to be a challenge. She was two days behind already. Poppy thought about sending a wire regarding the delay and informing him she would arrive shortly.

"Yeah, I've heard that for some time now. Where exactly are you headed?"

"Wouldn't you like to know?"

Noah shrugged.

She couldn't quite figure him out. He'd mentioned his ties to Molly and how he'd been hired to track down the strongboxes, but was that all he knew? She eyed him. She wasn't so sure. He was a Pinkerton after all.

"I know you're headed to Jefferson."

Poppy raised a brow.

"You told me in the restaurant before you poisoned me."

"You really do need to get over that. I had no choice. Besides, you lived."

"Barely." He took another drink of water. "Paul Malone."

She snapped her head toward him. How did he know the name? She hadn't mentioned him in any of their conversations. She was sure of it.

"You know him?" he asked.

She wasn't going to be baited this easy. "Nope."

"Hmmm...Jefferson City to meet Paul Malone."

Poppy lost all logic on staying quiet and blurted, "How in the hell do you know that?"

"I know a lot of things."

"Give it up, Pinkerton. Tell me how in blazes you know Paul Malone and that I'm to meet him in Jefferson?"

She watched as his dark eyes narrowed and his whiskered cheeks lifted into a grin.

"Paul Malone is Molly's brother."

"How do you know this?"

He held up his hand to quiet her.

"You have something to give him."

Shit. She'd been conned this whole time. Noah knew all about Molly, Paul, and the key.

He sighed and walked Bandit toward her. "I've decided to come clean." The sincerity in his eyes was enough to melt her heart.

"Why now?"

"Wolf Blackstone."

"What does he have to do with you being honest?"

"He has a lot to do with it." He straightened his wide shoulders. "If we are speaking about honesty, I'd say you fall in the dishonest category too."

"I haven't lied to you. I just haven't told you everything."

"Same here."

She nodded as they forged a silent acceptance of each other.

"Do you know what the key opens?" he asked.

She shook her head.

"A lock box. I'm hoping Paul knows which one."

"How do you know Paul?" she asked.

"About six months ago the agency contacted Molly in regard to the strongboxes being stolen. The government suspected her husband, Isaac Schmidt, manager of the First National Bank in St. Louis. Though it took some convincing, Molly was able to get us documents and wires of Isaac's correspondents with Lyle Clemmons."

"How does someone like Molly's husband get tied up with Lefty Clemmons?"

"They're cousins. Molly had placed the information into a lock box, and she had the key." He paused to point at the necklace around Poppy's neck. "Is that hers?"

She instinctively reached for the chain and fingered the brass key.

"Yes," she whispered.

"When Molly was killed, I'd hoped to find the key on her, but there was nothing. Seeing as you were the last one to be with her, I followed your trail and intercepted the wire before you sent it to Paul Malone."

"Pretty sneaky, Pinkerton."

"Just doing my job."

"Still doesn't explain how you knew Paul was Molly's brother."

"I'm a Pinkerton, Poppy—it is our job to investigate. Do you think I was going to let you walk into a trap? We needed to know who Malone was for various reasons and concerns."

She let out a long miserable sigh. How dumb had she been? It was clear she was a terrible bounty hunter, a farce. It had taken her this long to clue in to why he'd been with her all this time. It was his job.

"I was hired to track you down and see what you might know about the day Molly and Tad died, and if you had the key."

"You knew I had the key—you read the wire."

Noah shook his head.

"I did not know. You only stated that you had something for Paul from Molly. It could've been anything."

"Molly asked me to get the key to Paul Malone. She never said he was her brother, but then, she hadn't much time left." She fretted with her hat, remembering the way the little boy had felt in her arms...when the realization of who had killed them struck Poppy right in the heart.

She gasped. "Her husband—he's the one."

All the pieces started to fit, and she replayed the day when she found the mother and son. It was a clear spring afternoon, and the trees and fields had begun to wake from their winter sleep, as sprigs of green, yellow, and purple sprouted. Lost in the beauty of Mother Nature, Poppy rounded a bend in the road, then saw the turned-over wagon and pink gingham waving in the light breeze. A lead ball settled in her stomach, and she swallowed against the certainty that something terrible had happened.

Molly insisted Poppy pull her skirt up, and with bloodstained hands, the girl fumbled with the fabric until her fingers touched on an extra piece of cloth sewn into the seam. *Take it to Paul Malone, in Jefferson City.* After Poppy agreed, that's when Molly begged her to bring Tad and lay him in her arms. She glanced up at Noah, who watched her, concern and affection in his eyes. No, it couldn't be. They were complete opposites, and quite frankly she was fine being alone. The back of her neck ached at the lies she told herself.

"If the agency gets ahold of those papers, Isaac Schmidt will be hung."

"How could he kill his own wife and child?" She couldn't stop the angry tears as they fell from her eyes.

"He didn't want to get caught, is my guess, and he suspected her of deceiving him."

She wiped her eyes with the sleeve of her flannel shirt. "You won't need to worry about no papers. I'm gonna kill the son of a bitch."

"Now, hold on, hellcat. We need to settle things with Blackstone first and let the agency do their job when it comes to Schmidt."

Poppy's eyes overflowed with tears, and the lines on her face turned downward into an angry glare.

"Do you think Isaac hired Blackstone?"

"Yup, I do."

"How would he know anything about me?"

"When you brought Molly and Tad into St. Louis to the doctor's office, you told the doctor your name. That's how I was able to track you. Isaac must've done the same thing…and he knows you have the key."

"How would he know that? Molly gave it to me when I found them. No one else was around."

"My guess is Isaac knew Molly had the key on her— and that explains another reason they were killed."

"The Clemmons were looking for the key but didn't find it."

"That's right."

"I'm still going to kill him."

"We need to get the key to Paul and see if he has the box."

"And if he doesn't?"

"We will lasso that horse when we get there."

CHAPTER SEVEN

Low-lying clouds covered the stars and only a small portion of the moon peeked through. Poppy shivered involuntarily at the unnerving dark sky and glanced at Noah beside her. His Stetson sat lopsided on top of his head, and the hair on his face had grown a considerable amount since she'd first met him. He looked like hell, and she was sure she looked no better.

With Blackstone still tracking them, they'd stopped once on their trek to Jefferson, and it wasn't for more than a half hour to rest before they were in the saddles again. Her backside ached, and her legs had started to cramp. She flexed sore calves the same time her stomach gave a loud grumble.

"You should've eaten the rest of the rabbit," he said without looking at her.

She was on her last nerve. Tired, sore, and damn

hungry, she didn't need to be told what to do. She disregarded him and rubbed the wound on her shoulder. The skin had scabbed and itched like crazy. Most days she was able to ignore it, but in the evenings, she'd let loose in her sleep and scratch the crusted layer of skin right off, waking to a bloody mess.

Noah had gathered enough pinesap to last a month and insisted she lather the cut twice a day. He'd pestered her about infection and gangrene to the point where she was close to shooting him. She'd never tell him he was right; it'd just make him gloat. And, well, she couldn't guarantee she wouldn't injure him then. She knew all about infections and such from growing up with a doctor and Fern. She'd been keeping a close eye on the wound, looking for the telltale signs trouble was about to start. So far everything was healing up nice, even when she scratched it open. In between lathering her skin with the sap, she'd rubbed some of her sister's calendula oil into the cut for added insurance.

The lamps of Jefferson City came into view as they crested a hill. Noah had suggested they come into town at night, and she agreed. Blackstone was still out there, and by what they'd seen so far, he was a few steps ahead of them.

Noah led Bandit behind the livery and Poppy followed. The tinny sound of a piano floated off the rooftops toward them, and Milo snuffed.

"It's okay, boy. Soon you'll be resting on a bed of hay with a belly full of oats."

"We better steer clear of the saloon," Noah whispered.

She nodded.

Any trouble to be had, was sure to come from there. They walked their horses quietly along the small path behind the mercantile until they reached the livery.

"We're going to need to stay in the shadows. Without the horses it'll be easier to make it to the hotel unnoticed."

Noah knocked on the door of the small house attached to the livery. Poppy held the reins of both horses a step behind him.

A boy about fourteen came to the door.

"Is your pa home?" Noah asked.

"I'm the man of the house, sir, and if you're lookin' to board your horses, it's me who will do it."

He spoke clearly and in a tone that resonated no messing around. She squinted to get a better look at the young man. It wasn't unusual for women to be widowed at a young age and left with children to rear on their own. Some had a love affair with whiskey, which didn't bode well for the families they had, while others worked the fields until they died. She wondered if this boy's pa had favored the drink, or maybe he was a good man who taught his son about life and such things.

The closer she looked, the more she could see. His eyes were sharp and bright, but it was the line that held his mouth shut that she zeroed in on. The lips turned downward, and he clenched his teeth together, causing his front ones to lie crooked. When he moved his neck, she saw the scar at his collar slash across his throat. She'd bet the boy's pa had placed that mark on his skin, and if she was to guess any more, she'd wager he didn't take too kindly to keeping care of the livery either.

It was a sad life this boy led, and she wondered if he had brothers and sisters to care for as well.

"A brushing and oats are extra," the young man said.

"Give them one scoop in the morning and another in the evening." Noah handed him four greenbacks.

The boy glanced at the bills and then back to Noah. "You've given too much."

"I've given enough until the end of the week."

"There's more here than that." The boy's blond brows slanted. "I don't need your charity, mister."

"Kid, the extra cash is insurance if I need more days—that's all." Noah didn't wait for the boy's response; instead, he grabbed Poppy's hand and walked away.

"Don't let this go to your head, but I'm proud of you," Poppy said.

"For what?"

"For lookin' past the boy's pride to the sorrow beneath."

"Don't know what you're talkin' about."

He wouldn't take her compliment and she was fine with it, but he wasn't bamboozling her.

"You're a liar, Noah Shaw," she whispered.

His smile shone bright in the dark night.

CHAPTER EIGHT

"Not one word, Noah Shaw."

The look Poppy gave him was enough to set his skin afire, but he couldn't help himself and let out a loud whistle. The pale-green blouse was cut just below her chin, buttoned up tight, and tucked into a darker-green skirt. She was a sight all right. One of the most attractive women he'd ever laid eyes on. The long red mane was braided loosely at her nape and hung down to the middle of her back. She'd pulled the hair over to the side, covering the white streak completely.

"You don't even look the same." He probably shouldn't have said what he was thinking out loud, but it was too late—the words had passed, and he couldn't take them back.

Her scowl deepened. She reached for her Colts, no doubt to shoot him, but her hands came up empty. If she was to play the part of his wife, she couldn't look at all like the bounty hunter she was. No guns and no denims. She'd fought him on the whole idea this morning. There was no way Poppy Montgomery was wearing a dress. After a lot of cuss words and some foot stomping, she'd put on the skirt and blouse.

It was better this way. Now they could walk freely among the town without worrying about Blackstone taking shots at them. No one would suspect the fearless redhead to be dressed as a lady, and with her trademark white ribbon of hair hidden, she looked every bit the part.

"We need to blend in like everyone else. Blackstone could be among the crowd as we speak." He glanced out the window, turned back toward her, and smiled. "See, I've changed too." He held his arms open to display the tanned cotton shirt and dusty blue jeans he wore.

"I don't give a hog's tail what you look like. I can't breathe in this blasted corset, and the collar is itching the heck out of my chin." She scratched at her neck and wobbled, almost losing her balance. "And these shoes are atrocious."

He'd bought the fancy ankle-high boots from the shoemaker two streets over from the hotel and figured she'd like them. He should've known better. Poppy was only comfortable in a button shirt, slacks, and the worn, beat-up, leather boots with the patched wooden heel that sat beside the bed.

"Well, I think you look lovely," he said, trying to brighten the scowl on her face.

"Oh bah!" She swatted at the air, hiked up her skirt, and strapped a small derringer to her thigh.

Noah's jaw hung open at the sight of her snowy-white thigh. He swallowed and massaged his neck. Damn, the dress, the shoes, and now her long leg naked for him to see. He needed a drink.

He turned away from her and stared out the window. The more time he spent with Poppy gave way to more temptation to kiss the hell out of her. If he wasn't careful, she'd be in his arms and on the bed. He shook his head, trying desperately to clear the images of her sprawled out before him—a feast for the taking.

"I'm ready."

He faced her, and damn it if she didn't take his breath away, again. *Easy now.* He inhaled and pushed his lips into a smile.

"Indeed, Mrs. Shaw." He extended his elbow.

"I have to hold on to you too?"

"It's what married people do."

"It's not what I do." She stepped away from him.

Noah knew it was difficult for her to trust anyone. Her tough exterior told him she'd been hurt before, but he wasn't ever going to hurt her. Ruse or not, he'd protect her with his life.

"I promise all will be well, Poppy." He extended his arm again, and this time she took it. Her unease seeped from her body into his.

"Let's get this over with," she grumbled.

He led her to the door, holding her close, when it struck him that he didn't want his time with her to end. Once she handed the key to Paul and they took care of Blackstone, there was no reason for her to stay. He'd go back to the old routine of tracking killers, investigating bank frauds and the like, and she'd go back to collecting bounties. Was it any way to live? He wasn't too sure now that he'd met her, kissed her, and formed a bond with her. Noah knew he wasn't experiencing all the things he wanted to, and damn it if he didn't want to experience life with her.

Noah followed behind her as they walked down the long hallway of the Grant Hotel to the lobby. He kept a steady watch as Poppy's ankles wobbled and she stopped to regain her balance.

"You okay?" he asked.

She ignored him, straightened her shoulders and continued on.

When they entered the lobby, the foyer was busy with all sorts of people, from maids to butlers to customers. He tightened his hold on Poppy's arm. He never liked crowds. A ranch out in an open field far from town was what he'd always wanted, and, looking at Poppy out of the corner of his eye, he wondered if she'd wanted the same thing.

"Where is Paul's office?" she leaned in to ask as they walked out onto the boardwalk.

The scent of lavender wafted toward him, and he found himself leaning into her.

She pulled away and raised a brow.

"You smell nice."

"My sister insists I have some lavender oil with me at all times."

"I'm beginning to like your sister."

"Easy, Pinkerton—she's taken. And Gabe will shoot a hole right through your chest if you even look at her wrong."

"I take it Gabe is her husband?"

"And sheriff of Manchester—oh, and might I add he's good with a gun too."

"You trying to scare me?"

"Is it working?"

He smiled. "A little bit."

"Good, 'cause I ain't foolin' when it comes to my sister and the way Gabe feels about her."

He decided to change the subject, seeing as how her cheeks glowed and the line of her jaw clenched.

"Paul's office is a five-minute walk from the hotel."

She remained silent.

Noah got the feeling he'd struck a nerve with Poppy when it came to her sister, and if things were different, he'd explain she was the one he wanted.

He sighed. Another time. The boardwalk ended, and they stepped onto the street and walked past more stores.

Poppy stumbled, and he tightened his hold on her so she didn't fall. The shoes had been a bad idea; he could see that now. And from what he'd witnessed so far with the redhead, she'd make him pay for it, too.

"It's right there. I see the sign," she said and pointed at the wooden board hanging above the door.

He glanced at the people around them. Two cowboys lounged beside the bakery window; both stopped their conversation to stare at Poppy as she walked by. Noah clamped his molars together. She didn't belong to him, but that didn't stop him from wanting to protect her from everything, and that included the two wranglers. He scrutinized every single person they passed, looking for any sign of trouble. For all he knew, Blackstone had others working for him like he'd done with the Hatt boys.

Noah took one last look around before he opened the door to Paul's office, allowing Poppy entrance before he followed.

Poppy stepped inside, the smell of freshly oiled wood accosted her. She refrained from covering her nose but couldn't help the face she made. The wood walls glistened, as did the desk sitting in the corner. The space was small—all things considered—and figured there were more rooms in the back for storage and living quarters.

The door to their left opened, and Poppy spotted a stove and table with two chairs. She'd been right. He resided where he worked.

"May I help you?" the man asked.

"Mr. Malone?"

"Why, yes. I am Paul Malone, and you might be?" He reached out his hand to Noah first.

She stiffened. Men were of higher rank than a woman when it came to most things, but darn it if the simple gesture of shaking Noah's hand before hers didn't get Poppy's blood boiling.

"Noah Shaw, Pinkerton."

Paul's skin paled, and his eyes darted to the door and back to Noah. He smiled showing all of his teeth.

"Welcome. What can I do for you?"

She scrutinized the lawyer's shuffling feet and wide pupils. Poppy reached for her side but remembered she wasn't carrying her Colts. Instead of drawing unwanted attention to herself, she rubbed her midsection.

"This is Poppy Montgomery. She sent you a telegraph about your sister."

She placed a smile on her face and bowed her head slightly.

"Yes, it is a pleasure, Miss Montgomery, to finally make your acquaintance." He reached out his hand, and she reluctantly allowed him to take it in his own.

She didn't miss the shift in his stance or the way his eyes roamed her face.

"You do not resemble a bounty hunter, Miss Montgomery."

"Call me Poppy."

He shrugged. "If that is what you wish, Poppy." He ushered them toward his desk. "Please, sit."

She didn't want to sit. The corset pushed on her ribs, and she couldn't imagine the discomfort if she were to bend. She'd likely pass out before she heard a word Paul said. She would have remained standing, but Noah pressed his hands into her shoulders and gently forced her into the chair. She glared at him as he took the seat beside her.

"I am sorry about your sister and nephew," Noah said.

"Thank you—it is such a shame." He pulled out the chair and sat across from them.

"Do you know any of the details of how they were murdered?" Poppy asked.

"Sadly, I do. Isaac sent me a letter."

"And what did Mr. Schmidt say?" Noah asked before Poppy had the chance to.

"They were ambushed by some outlaws."

"Yeah, his damn cousin!" Poppy blurted.

"We don't know that for sure." Noah leaned in. "Personally, I think it was random. Just happened to be in the wrong place—know what I mean?"

What the hell was Noah doing? He knew damn-well that Lefty was Isaac's cousin. He'd told her so.

"Are you tracking the outlaws, Mr. Shaw?" Paul asked.

"Well, we were, but the agency has long given up on them."

Paul glanced at Poppy, and she knew he wondered how the two had come to be together if not for the obvious.

"I hunted Poppy down when we were trying to apprehend the outlaws who killed Molly and Tad. Since the job has been called off, I decided to come here with her," Noah explained.

Paul seemed to like the answer he gave and smiled. The beginning of a moustache framed his top lip. She wondered how old he was.

"What is it you have from my sister?" he asked.

She was reluctant to hand over the key, and instead of plopping the chain into his palm, she decided to lie.

"I have a key of some sort."

"I was hoping you'd say that." He sighed loudly. "Molly had come to visit a month before she passed and asked me to go with her to open a safe-deposit box. The banks in Jefferson don't have them. There is only one place in town, The Safe Deposit Company, where you can do so. However, rules are strict. The rent on the box must be paid for one full year up front, and the only person allowed access to it is the key holder."

Now she understood why Isaac needed the key. He couldn't get the box without it—the safe-deposit company wouldn't let him, and she was sure he'd tried. Whatever was in the box was far more valuable than some transcripts between the banker and the outlaw.

Poppy smiled at Molly's brother.

"I didn't bring the key with me; it's back at the hotel."

Paul frowned.

"We weren't sure if you'd be here," Noah interjected. "The hotel is only a couple of blocks away. We can head back and get it."

"I have some business to attend to this afternoon. Could you come by afterward?" Paul asked.

"What time would you prefer?"

"Does five o'clock suit you?"

Noah nodded and reached for Poppy's hand, but she pulled it away.

It took all her strength not to blast Noah in Paul's

office. She rubbed her molars together and squeezed her hands into tight fists. Noah and Paul had been talking as if she wasn't there. She was the one who'd contacted Paul, not Noah, and she was the one who had the key, damn it. If it wasn't for her, they wouldn't be here. Without so much as a word, she exited the office, letting the door slam behind her.

"What's gotten into you?" Noah asked, coming up behind her.

She quickened her pace to stay ahead of him, when her ankles began to wobble. She could feel herself falling forward. Poppy's arms flew out to catch her balance, but it was to no avail and she toppled forward, skirts and all. The wooden walk met her knees, jarring both legs. She'd have bruises for sure. Every curse word she knew hovered on the tip of her tongue, and she bit down hard on her cheek to keep from spewing them.

Noah reached underneath her armpits and pulled her up.

"Are you all right?"

The concern she saw in his brown eyes made her cringe with embarrassment. She had wanted some distance from him and his know-it-all attitude. He and Paul could go on their merry way, for all she was concerned. In fact, she'd give Noah the key, and he could do with it what he pleased. She was leaving this blasted city.

She shoved his hands from her.

"Whoa, Red, I just want to help."

"Like you did in there?" She walked past him, her feelings hurt and pride diminished. She was sure people stared at her clumsiness caused by the bloody shoes, but she didn't care. Her mission was to get as far from Noah as possible.

"Hold on. Why are you so hot and bothered?" he asked, walking beside her.

Not slowing her pace, she yanked the chain from around her neck, catching it on the button of her blouse. Poppy growled low and clamped her teeth together. She fidgeted with the chain until she had no patience left and yanked it from the blouse. The button flew off at the same time the necklace broke, and the key soared through the air.

Poppy froze.

Noah jumped onto the street and scooped up the metal key before it bounced into a pile of horse manure.

"What in hell has gotten into you?" he asked.

She could see the anger and irritation in the lines around his eyes. If he wanted a fight, she'd give it to him.

"Take the key. I'm leaving."

CHAPTER NINE

Noah examined every corner of her beautiful face, from the frown lines on her forehead to the pout of her lush lips. He wasn't sure what had gotten her all riled up, but he could see she would not back down. He didn't want to fight with her. He wanted to kiss her. He almost smiled but decided against it. She was still glaring at him. One thing he'd learned well since being with Poppy was her defiant nature and her determination to fight when she thought she was in the right. Now was one of those times.

"Have I done something to upset you?"

"Darn right you have, Noah Shaw." She dug her fingers into the collar of her blouse and scratched at her skin.

He reached for her hand.

She stepped backward.

"Please, tell me what I've done wrong." He could hear the whine in his own voice, and it irritated him, but Poppy was more important than his pride.

"You're no better than me just because you're a man."

Now he understood. She was peeved because Paul and he had discussed things without including her.

"I know you picked up on something in there. I saw it in your eyes, but what I also saw was your harsh mouth and short temper."

"How dare you!"

He took hold of her arm; this time she did not pull away from him. He needed to get her off of the street and away from Paul's office. Blackstone was still out there, and the lawyer had shown signs of distress. Which meant one thing: he couldn't be trusted.

Noah pulled her along behind him until they came to a shallow walkway between two buildings. Once out of sight from the citizens of Jefferson City, he released her.

"I sensed the same thing you did while in Paul's office."

"How do you know what I sensed?" she growled.

"C'mon, Poppy—you saw exactly what I did. Paul was nervous."

"I agree. He's not telling us something." The fire extinguished from her eyes, and her shoulders dropped.

The anger dissolved from her body now that he'd put her sights onto something else.

"Right. Now, let's go see what's in that box before we have to meet with Paul again."

"Hold on, Pinkerton. Why did you tell him the agency had called off their investigation of the Clemmons?"

"He couldn't know we were onto him. I wanted him to think we had no interest in the Clemmons or Isaac Schmidt." She nodded. "Are we going to stand here and chitchat or find out what's in that damn box?"

"You need the contents in the box for your investigation. Do we just take it?"

"That's the plan." He smiled.

Her lips lifted into a devilish grin, and Noah couldn't resist her any longer. He groaned low in his throat, hooked his arm around her waist, and pulled her to him. She had no time to refuse or push him from her, and he used her shock to his advantage.

Noah moved his lips over hers. Within seconds he wanted to devour her. Their kiss intensified into a battle of tongues. He wanted her—not just for today but for always. The soft moan coming from Poppy caused his stomach to tighten with anticipation. His body driven solely on the desire building between them, he cupped her breast, massaging the soft mound until the nipple hardened underneath the blouse.

Noah pressed his forehead into hers and released her

lips. He regretted it the moment the warm air caressed his lonesome mouth.

"I could kiss you all damn day," he breathed.

"Would make for an interesting day."

The lines on her face were straight, and he figured she hadn't known what to say. He kept his chuckle to himself, lest he hurt her feelings.

"*Interesting* doesn't even touch on what would happen, Red."

He felt her stiffen beneath him. He'd pushed her too far, and she was uncomfortable. It wasn't long before she wiggled out of his embrace and placed a few feet of distance between them.

She wound the fabric of her skirt around her fist. Her lips dark pink and swollen from his assault on them begged him to kiss her once more. His pants were uncomfortably tight, and he stepped to the side to loosen them. The citizens of Jefferson milled about on the boardwalk and street none the wiser of them tucked into a narrow hall between two buildings.

"We best get going," she said.

He smiled, fighting the need to hold her in his arms once more.

She went ahead of him and stepped out onto the busy street. Noah pointed left, and they walked in silence. He didn't dare touch her hand but flexed his fingers instead. Poppy had made it clear she wasn't comfortable. It was getting more difficult by the day to control his urges when he was around her. She'd nestled herself inside his cold and lonely heart, and, damn it, she wouldn't leave. He'd wait until things had been settled with Schmidt and Blackstone before he told Poppy how he felt.

The Safe Deposit Company of Jefferson came into view at the end of the block. Noah's hand automatically went to the revolver hanging on his hip. He'd forgotten to top up the revolver before they left the room, too overcome with Poppy's appearance. He remembered the extra bullets he'd left on the nightstand when they were in Paul's office, and the lawyer had become nervous and squirmy. Not one to leave himself short on bullets, he chalked up the forgetfulness to his recent craving for Poppy. Hell, he'd better get himself together. Now was not the time to go all soft. Wolf Blackstone was out there, and Noah was sure the bounty hunter was close. As a Pinkerton he had a job to do, and the agency was counting on him to bring them the evidence they needed.

Noah took a deep fortifying breath, placed his hand on the butt of the Peacemaker, and gripped the handle tight.

Poppy planted her feet so she didn't run for the hills. Noah had provoked feelings inside her heart that she was sure did not exist any longer. Over the years bounty hunting she'd built a barrier around her soul, not letting anyone close, even her sisters.

Thinking of Fern and Ivy caused her eyes to well. She missed them terribly. Living the life she did was not for the weak, and even though she was as tough as hell, she wished for finer things. And whether she'd admit it to anyone or not, she wanted to be loved like her sister was by Gabe.

Noah held the door open to the Security Deposit Company. She placed a smile upon her face and scanned the room with a bounty hunter's eye. The building was not as big as it looked from the outside. Two doors stood together in the corner of the room. A young man in a suit, no older than Ivy, kept watch. He wore the coat open to display the Remingtons on his hips.

She'd seen this before. It was an act to show he was armed and he'd shoot if provoked. Poppy glanced at the young man's face again. Patchy whiskers checkered his cheeks and chin. Long hair combed back to touch the collar of his shirt. The young fellow's hands drew her gaze from his face. His long fingers and wide palms shook. She'd bet the greenbacks in her saddlebag that he hadn't been at the job for very long, and he hadn't the fortitude to shoot someone.

She figured the deposit boxes must be behind the

door he guarded. She felt sorry for the young man. He would die doing his job. If the place was ever robbed, the boy didn't have enough experience to know what to do.

Noah placed his hand on the small of her back and guided her to the line of people waiting either to deposit or remove items from their boxes. She grew nervous. Her neck ached, and a large lump formed in her throat.

"What do you suggest we do?" she whispered.

"It's your box, Poppy. You've just come to retrieve it." He grabbed her hand and put the key inside her palm.

She chewed on the inside of her cheek. The long skirt felt as if it were made of lead and pulled her slowly to the ground. Her chest tightened.

"You've killed outlaws. This is way easier," Noah whispered.

"I don't know about that."

"You can do this."

The line moved and they stepped forward.

She patted at her hair, fixing the red ribbon to cover the white band.

"Relax, Red. Your hair looks beautiful."

"I don't need your compliments, Noah Shaw. I need a damn drink of water and my bloody Colts."

The guns calmed her even in the most harried moments. If she had them all would be well, and Poppy could finish any job. But right now, she was without them, and it made her uneasy.

"I've got my pistol."

"I'm a better shot."

Noah chuckled. "Doubt that."

She gave him a sideways glance. "I'd bet my horse on it."

Noah's eyes grew big. "You'd bet Milo?"

"I'd sure as heck would."

"It'd be a shame to lose your old friend—but I'll take that bet." He put out his hand.

She hesitated only because of her choice as leverage for the bet, but his confidence irritated her and she shook his hand.

Poppy sighed. She couldn't back down now, and she wouldn't lose her horse. She'd win the damn bet no matter what.

The man in front of them moved, and it was their turn to walk up to the desk. Poppy forced her feet to step forward.

"May I help you?" a man with circle glasses and a bushy brown mustache asked.

"Um…yes, I have a box I'd like to see," Poppy said.

"Do you have the key?"

She placed Molly's key on the counter. The man scooped it up and held it close to his eyes.

"Number twenty-nine," he said. "Box twenty-nine?"

Noah poked her in the ribs.

"I'm sorry, yes…it is twenty-nine."

"Your name, ma'am?"

"Pop—"

Noah coughed.

She glanced at him.

"Go ahead, Molly dear."

Her eyes grew wide. Shoot! She'd almost said her name instead of Molly's. Thanks to Noah and his sensibility, she'd been saved.

"Molly Schmidt," she said.

The man nodded and turned a ledger toward her.

"Please sign here."

She took the feathered pen from him, dipped it in the inkwell, and scribbled Molly's name. He smiled, held his arm out toward the doors that led to the boxes, and bid them good afternoon.

Noah took her hand and tugged her in the direction of the young guard and the secrets that lay behind the wall. She was thankful he did, too. Her legs felt like a newborn calf's, and had he not been holding on to her, she was sure to fall right on her face.

The boy at the door did not make eye contact with them, and she figured it was from his inexperience and age. It was a shame. If there had been time, she'd have told him to always make eye contact, know your assailant and, in this case, know your thief.

She stepped into the room and was a bit surprised to see it was nothing special. Small metal boxes covered two walls and stood a foot from the ceiling. The room exuded the musty scent of stale air and body odor. There were no windows to let air and light into the room, and she wondered how the other patrons were able to see their documents.

Poppy made her way to the first row of boxes. They weren't very big, and she wondered what kind of things people placed in such a tiny hole. It didn't take her long to figure out the cases were numbered with a brass marker starting at the top row with the number one. She followed the numbers with her eyes.

"Box twenty-nine is right here," Noah said, pointing to a marker in the middle of the wall, third row from the top.

Poppy tried not to look anxious and slowly walked toward him. She slid the key into the lock and turned. The latch clicked, and she opened the door. Her lungs stilled while she pulled the papers out from the small hole in the wall. Noah stood back waiting for her to place them onto the narrow counter standing behind them.

Unable to read the papers, she turned up the lamp. Still no better, she squinted to decipher the words. The first four papers were telegrams scribbled in messy handwriting, and after waiting for her eyes to adjust to the dim light, she was able to read them.

"You were right. Isaac was corresponding with Clemmons to rob the stages." She passed him the stack of handwritten notes with locations, dates, and times of where Wells Fargo and other stages would be. The bank manager was making a mint pulling off these heists.

"There has to be more." Noah reached for the other papers she'd not gone through yet.

"What are you looking for?"

"I'll know when I find it."

He'd forgotten one. The folded piece of paper could've easily been missed had she not seen it stuck to the back of one of the letters from Clemmons. She pulled the paper apart to reveal a map.

"What on earth…?" she whispered.

Noah leaned over her shoulder; his nearness unsettled her stomach, and she shivered.

"You're looking at a map of the railroad—or soon-to-be railroad."

"What do you mean?" She couldn't decipher anything from the map other than where St. Louis was, and only because the name of the city was written on the paper.

"See this line here? That is where the railroad wants to go." He rifled through more of the papers. "Look at these."

Poppy leaned closer.

"These are deeds to land, and they're not owned by

Isaac." He shifted more papers to show her. "But these ones say they are."

"What do those have to do with the railroad?"

"By the looks of things, Isaac was stealing the deeds and forging them as his. He was selling them to the railroad."

"He was not only taking people's money but their land as well?"

"That's right, Red."

Poppy's mouth gaped as the truth sank in.

"That explains why he killed his wife."

"And why he's hired Wolf Blackstone to kill you." His statement sobered her. She'd almost forgotten about the deadly bounty hunter.

"What do we do now?" she asked.

"We put the papers back and inform the agency."

She helped him shove the documents back inside the compartment, when an envelope addressed to Paul written in dainty handwriting fell to the floor. She scooped it up and slipped it into the pocket of her skirt before locking the box. She gripped the key within her hand and followed Noah out into the common area.

He stepped in front of her and halted.

"What are you doing?"

"Stay behind me." His voice was low and unchallenging, and she knew it meant trouble.

CHAPTER TEN

Poppy peered around Noah's shoulder and came face-to-face with Wolf Blackstone. She dropped the key into the pocket sewn into her skirt.

"Afternoon, folks," the bounty hunter said. There was no mistaking the friendly words for anything but what they were: deadly.

"Wolf," Noah said, his hand hovering over the gun strapped to his side.

"Unless you want a bullet in your chest, Shaw, I suggest you move away from the pistol."

Noah eased his hand into Poppy's and pulled her closer.

"You gonna shoot us right here in broad daylight and in the middle of the Security Deposit Company?" she snipped.

Wolf's thin lips lifted into a deadly smile.

"Don't much care where I kill you."

"What do you want, Blackstone?" she asked.

Wolf's eyes were the color of metal, and in them she saw nothing. No remorse, no empathy, no kindness. She was beginning to see why Noah was so adamant they stay far away from him. Poppy stood taller. The bounty hunter may have been good at his job, but she was better, and if she had her guns, she'd show him.

"I'm not here for you," he said to Noah.

"I go where she does."

"I don't need you. I'll be fine," she said to Noah. Her effort to brush him aside didn't work when he turned and glared at her. She'd never forgive herself if something happened to him. This was not his fight. It was hers and, damn it, he wasn't invited. She shoved him away from her.

"Go on. I'm tired of you hoverin' over me like a crow scavengin' for food. I'm capable of taking care of myself." She changed the angles of her face to show no remorse for her words, even when he stared at her in disbelief. She'd hurt him, and he'd never know how much it broke her heart to do it, but he wouldn't die because of her.

"She's a bit of a pain in the ass. You still set on takin' her?" Noah asked Wolf.

The hired killer nodded; his eyes penetrated into Poppy's.

She gave him a cold stare of her own, but he never flinched. He'd be a tough one to take down, and she'd be surprised if she didn't end up with a bullet wound or two.

"I'll take you both." Wolf motioned for them to walk ahead of him and out into the bright afternoon sun and bustling street.

"Where exactly are we going?" Noah asked.

"Malone's office."

Bloody hell. She'd known Paul Malone was involved in this. Poppy's temper rose, and her cheeks heated. The damn skirt caught between her legs, and she stumbled. Noah grabbed her forearm, and she shrugged his hold from her. It was best if she kept him at a distance—it might save his life.

They walked side by side, Blackstone close behind them. She surveyed the people in front of her and beside her, the buildings and the carriages passing by. There was nowhere for them to go. She was desperate for a distraction—anything to help aid in their escape.

Poppy didn't have much time. Paul's office was at the end of the street. She refrained from showing any signs of distress. instead, she concentrated on an escape. The distraction she needed had just come around the corner: two horses and one rider.

"I will kill him if you take one step to the left." Wolf's deep, ominous voice carried toward her.

In the ten minutes she'd been in Blackstone's company, he'd shown her just how good he was at his job. She shifted to the right and into Malone's office. The oiled wood hit her senses like it had the first time, and she reached up to cover her nose. Wolf cocked his gun.

"You seem a little edgy," she snapped. "Possibly due to nerves?"

"I don't get nervous or edgy," Wolf replied.

She shrugged.

"I say you're lyin'."

"Poppy," Noah growled.

She knew he wanted her to be quiet, but with Wolf's reaction to her insults, there was no way she'd let up now.

"I'd say you're yellow," she crowed.

Wolf slammed the cold steel of his Remington to her forehead.

Poppy clenched her jaw, and her eyes watered from the pain.

"There's a price on your head, bitch, and I plan on collecting it." His teeth pressed together, and saliva gathered in the corner of his lips. "How yellow am I if I blast a hole in your head right here?"

"You won't do it." She pushed her forehead into the barrel. "I heard about how you let Lefty and his boys walk away from a robbery last month."

He growled low in his throat, and his eyes turned black.

"Seems you ain't a bounty hunter after all but a damn coward." She knew now he must've been on Schmidt's payroll to let such a thing happen.

He wrapped his gloved hand into the braid hanging down her back and yanked. The Remington dented her flesh, but her eyes never left his.

She knew Noah would go for his Peacemaker and heard the barrel cock behind them.

"Let her go, Wolf."

Blackstone swung the Remington away from her flesh toward Noah, and fired.

Poppy screamed. She didn't think the bounty hunter would shoot. She rammed her elbow into Wolf's stomach. He slumped forward, loosening his hold on her, and she lunged toward Noah. Poppy dropped to her knees. Blood seeped onto his chest. She panicked. She gripped the cotton shirt and tore it open. Buttons flew onto the floor, hitting the hardwood, and rolled under the desk.

"I'm okay, Red—it's just my arm," Noah said between short breaths.

"Are you sure?" She continued to feel his bare chest, ribs, and stomach, looking for any other gunshot wounds.

"I'm sure."

She glanced at him and their eyes locked. At that moment she could not imagine a day without him. She loved him. Aw hell, she bloody well loved him.

Poppy almost grimaced at the newfound feelings. Instead, she averted her gaze and inspected his shoulder.

Wolf kicked her out of the way and removed Noah's holster along with his revolvers. He tossed them onto Paul's desk, all while keeping his gun trained on her.

A piece of bone protruded from the top part of Noah's shoulder. She closed her eyes to block the sudden surge of nausea crawling up her throat. People passed by the window. She wondered if Wolf had locked the door.

She swiveled toward the bastard, but her eyes went past him to Paul tied to his desk chair, a piece of rag stuffed in his mouth. Molly's brother hadn't been involved in the raids after all. It explained why he'd been offish when they'd come in earlier. Wolf must've been here, but when Poppy said she didn't have the key, he'd changed his plan and followed them.

She turned back toward Noah, bent and placed a light kiss to his lips. She reached for his hand and eased it up her skirt. His eyes shot open, shock and surprise swimming within the dark pools, but she ignored him and continued the kiss.

"Stand up or I'll kill him," said Blackstone.

She left Noah's side and faced their attacker. "You're here for the key, and you're gonna take my life along with it."

"You're a smart one,"

"I'll make you a deal. Shoot me like a real man and not like a coward, and you get both of the things you've come here for."

He shifted, jutting his chest outward.

She didn't miss the way his hand flexed around the handle of his Remington. He was cunning and devious—two things that didn't sit well with any bounty hunter.

"If you're as fast as you say, this should be easy for you." She could see he was thinking about it, and she played on his ego and reputation. "Surely you can beat a woman."

"I could beat you with my eyes closed."

"True, you could. All I ask is that you give me the chance to go out with some dignity instead of being shot in the back."

"I forbid you to do this, Poppy," Noah wheezed. He'd shimmied himself up the wall into a sitting position.

"Don't care, Shaw." She refused to look at him.

"Damn it, Poppy. You're not good enough. You cannot win against someone like him."

"Be quiet. You don't know me or nothin' about me."

Now was not the time for him to be second-guessing her. As it was, she didn't know if she'd beat the bastard on her own.

"You have no gun," Wolf said.

She glanced down at Noah. "I'll use his."

Wolf nodded.

The holster was a bit too big for her waist, but with the skirt and bustle underneath, she could make do. She chose the pistol that would fit her left hand the best and kneaded the ivory handle within her palm.

"Where do you want to do this, Blackstone?" She faced him.

"Right here, but first put the key on the desk."

She shifted the Colt on her hip, dug her hand into the pocket, pulled out the key, and slapped it onto the counter.

Paul groaned from the chair across the room, a look of despair settled on his handsome face. She didn't know if the truth of what had happened to his sister had entered his mind, or if it was what she might have placed in the box that had the tears falling from his eyes. It was the only thing he had left of her, and Poppy let the remorse for him wrap around her heart. She couldn't let Wolf have the key. He couldn't win.

Poppy inhaled.

She walked to the center of the room, placed her feet shoulder-width apart, and faced Blackstone. She waited.

Her hand hovered over the butt of the Peacemaker. The room was still, the air musty, and a rainbow of colors shone in through the window to dance on the wooden floor. She didn't dare let anything or anyone distract her from the target ahead of her. He'd shoot the minute her guard was down.

Wolf kept his hands at his sides, his stance wide, and his eyes cold.

CHAPTER ELEVEN

Noah's heart lodged in his throat. All he could do was watch Poppy's display of courage. A part of him wanted to close his eyes and not see what was about to happen; the other desperately wanted to shield her from the bullet he knew would strike her flesh.

He only had one chance to help her, and if he failed, Blackstone would not only kill Poppy but Noah, too. The room held an eerie silence while the two bounty hunters faced off. The timing needed to be exact—to the point and right on the letter. Any false move from him and he'd be showered with bullets.

Sweat trickled down his temple and into the hair on his cheeks. No sudden moves. Be still. He scrutinized Wolf; the bounty hunter's first finger closest to the trigger twitched. Noah's breath froze within his lungs…and then all hell broke loose.

Poppy was quick. The gun was out, cocked, and fired all within seconds. Three shots went off, and when the smoke cleared, Poppy and Wolf lay on the ground.

Shit! He dove toward her, ignoring the ache in his shoulder.

"Red!" He rolled her over. Blood dripped from a slash across her left cheek. It took her some time to open her eyes. Then, the green pools peered up at him, and he was lost. He gently brushed a lock of hair from her forehead.

There was nothing else. No life to live if it was without her.

"How're you feeling?" he asked.

The sun-kissed cheeks grew bright until they glowed red.

"You should've aimed for his chest, Shaw." She shoved him from her and sat up.

"I aimed for his gun. If I hadn't, you'd be dead right now." She swayed to the left, and he reached for her, but she slapped his hand away. "I thought—"

"I know damn well what you thought. You figured me dead." She stood and went to Blackstone, who lay on the ground unmoving "You didn't trust I'd beat him."

He couldn't deny her accusations. When she'd knelt down and kissed him after he'd gotten shot, she'd brazenly stuck his hand up her skirt. At first Noah was taken aback at her forthrightness, but when his fingers skimmed the small derringer strapped to her thigh, he clued in awfully fast.

"I had a pocket revolver. You know as good as I do how inaccurate they are. I was lucky enough to hit his hand, and you were damn lucky his bullet grazed your cheek because of it." He tried to reason with her.

Wolf Blackstone lay on his back, a gunshot wound to his forehead and one to his right hand.

"See, you killed him," Noah said.

She gave him an icy stare.

He reached for her, and to his surprise she went into his arms willingly.

"What matters is you're alive." He kissed her forehead.

"I suppose." She sighed.

He brushed his lips against hers.

Paul groaned from behind them, and Noah remembered the lawyer. He took the letter opener on the desk and cut the rope from around Paul's wrists.

Once the man had removed the cloth from his mouth, he grabbed Poppy's hand.

"Thank you. Thank you so much." His brown eyes were wide, and his hair disheveled.

"Are you okay?" Poppy asked.

Paul nodded, but Noah wasn't too sure. The man had just witnessed someone die. Not all people were pulled from the same cotton, and Paul wasn't accustomed to such violence.

"You sure?" Noah asked.

"I've never seen anyone shoot that fast," Paul said to Poppy.

"She's quick."

"I have something for you," she said and handed Paul an envelope.

Noah cocked his eyebrow.

"Don't worry, Pinkerton—this letter is addressed to him. It won't interfere with the case."

Paul took the envelope, his hands shaking as he opened it. After reading it, he raised tear-soaked eyes to them.

"She knew he'd try to kill her, and she was asking me to take care of Tad."

"I'm sorry, Paul." Noah placed his hand on the man's shoulder.

"Will there be justice for my sister and nephew?" he asked.

"I can promise you Isaac Schmidt will be punished."

"I want him killed."

"I'll do it," Poppy said.

"The hell you will," Noah growled.

"I don't answer to you, Shaw."

He could see the determination in the fold of her brows and the grit flash in her eyes.

"It's a government case, Poppy."

"I'm a bounty hunter." She tipped her chin. "I don't give a damn about anything else."

Noah let out a long sigh. He wasn't going to win this one. Poppy wanted revenge for the young mother and her son. And so did he.

"I'll make you a deal," he said to her.

"I'm done making bets with you. I've learned my lesson."

"We hunt together."

"Absolutely not." She turned from him. "Rest assured, Mr. Malone, I will finish the job."

"Will you be alone?" Paul asked, concern on his young face.

Noah almost snickered. He could feel the anger radiate off Poppy. Instead of clearing out of there and away from her wrath, he pulled her into his arms. The muscles in her shoulders and back were tight, and he caressed the nape of her neck, working the anger from her body.

"I can't be without you, Poppy," he whispered into her ear.

She sighed, and he moved his lips along her jaw to the lush mouth he so desired.

"We make a great team," he said between short kisses.

"I work alone," she said against his lips.

"Not anymore."

She pressed into him, and he was lost.

CHAPTER TWELVE

"What do you mean he's dead?" Poppy yelled from atop her horse.

"The fellow inside the mercantile said there was a shoot-out yesterday, and Isaac Schmidt perished along with one of our agents," Noah said.

They'd left Jefferson City three days before and had only been in St. Louis a half hour when Noah insisted they stop at the mercantile to send a telegram to the Pinkerton Agency.

"Is he sure? Where is the body?" Poppy's cheeks heated, and she refrained from placing her hands upon them. How could they have been one day short? She eyed Noah, his arm in a makeshift sling from the gunshot wound days before. This was his fault.

"Schmidt's laid out behind the sheriff's, and the agent's casket was placed at the church."

"If we hadn't stopped in Clear Water, we would've made it on time," she snapped.

"Are you suggesting this to be my fault?"

"It sure as hell is."

He took off his hat, and his dark hair glistened in the sun.

"Damn it, Poppy."

"You slow me down. I told you I work alone."

"We work together," he growled.

She could see the anger crawl up his clean-shaven face, but she ignored the silent warning to back off.

"I didn't agree to nothin'."

"You didn't disagree either."

"This is your fault, Noah Shaw. My bullet should've killed Schmidt—not some bloody Pinkerton's."

"Aw, hell. And what if I'd have shot him? What then?"

"Don't flatter yourself. I'm faster and better."

"That has yet to be decided."

"It doesn't need to be. It's a fact."

"You think so?"

"Yup, have a nice life, Pinkerton—I'm leaving."

"The hell you are," Noah said.

He stepped toward Poppy, reached up with his good arm, and yanked her from Milo's back.

She stumbled, almost losing her footing, but Noah held onto her shirtsleeve.

"Release me at once!"

"Not until you get ahold of yourself." He gave her a little shake.

"Take your hands off of me, Pinkerton, or you'll be sorry." Noah chuckled, and the sound infuriated her. "You've gone loco, and that temper of yours needs to be contained."

Who the hell did he think he was, accosting her like this?

"I will not be told what to do by some badge-wearing highfalutin lawman."

"We ride together, Poppy, from now on. We do everything together." Noah's lips thinned.

No one gave her orders. She admired Noah and had fallen in love with him, but to hell if she'd be under his thumb.

"I am not your puppet. You do not hold my strings!" She shoved him from her, but he did not let go.

"I'm not sure how you've worked alone all this time without being killed. You're not a bounty hunter—you're a woman, and you need to act like one!"

Poppy's temper exploded. She hauled off and punched him square in the jaw. She watched as his head snapped to the side, but the grin he'd had never left his lips, and she stepped back.

Noah was quick, and she had no time to react when he spun her around and pushed her up against Milo's side. The cold metal wrapped around her wrist with a loud clink. He'd handcuffed her…to him!

"What are you doing?" she asked.

Noah stepped closer…a breath stood between them. She could smell the lye soap he'd used to shave this morning, and every part of her wanted to caress his cheek. How could his nearness cause such feelings inside her? She was immobile. Couldn't move even if she wanted to. She tried to hold on to her anger, but when he leaned in to place his lips to hers, she lost all reason and the fight seeped from her.

"I love you, Poppy Montgomery," he said against her lips. "And I ain't livin' another moment of my life without you."

She pressed into him, afraid he might see her tears.

"I know you love me, too," he said.

She closed her eyes, and the hot afternoon breeze dried her cheeks when he pulled away to look at her.

"Open your eyes."

"I can't," she whispered, too afraid for him to see how defenseless she was while in his arms.

"Look at me, Poppy, please."

There had been a yearning—hunger edged his voice, and the way he'd said her name made her open her eyes. Within the dark depths looking back at her, she witnessed a love so strong and sure she'd never have to second-guess him again. He'd never leave her.

"Say it," he whispered. When she thought of a life without him, her soul cried out in agony. "Say you love me, Red."

Unable to deny him—or his kisses—any longer, she placed her lips to his and whispered, "I love you with all of my heart, Noah Shaw."

MESSAGE FROM THE AUTHOR

Dear Reader,

I loved writing this book. Poppy Montgomery is a firecracker, and she meets her match when Pinkerton, Noah Shaw arrests her. I hope you enjoy this book as much as I did writing it.

Ivy's story will be out soon.

As always a huge thank you to my family without your support and understanding I would not be able to write the books I do. I love you!

God Bless!
Love,
Kat

About the Author

Kat Flannery's love of history shows in her novels. She is an avid reader of historical, suspense, paranormal, and romance. A member of many writing groups, Kat enjoys promoting other authors on her blog. She's been published in numerous periodicals throughout her career.

Her debut novel *CHASING CLOVERS* has been an Amazon bestseller many times. *LAKOTA HONOR* and *BLOOD CURSE* (Branded Trilogy) are Kat's two award-winning novels. Kat is currently hard at work on her next book.

When not researching for her next book, Kat can be found spending time with her three sons and husband.

RECEIVE KAT'S MONTHLY NEWSLETTER:
http://eepurl.com/cQmCzL
KAT'S WEBSITE: www.katflannerybooks.com
FACEBOOK: Kat Flannery, author
TWITTER: @KatFlannery1

www.ingramcontent.com/pod-product-compliance
Lightning Source LLC
Chambersburg PA
CBHW071310130626
46556CB00004B/1547

* 9 7 8 0 9 8 1 1 0 5 6 6 6 *